Tall Stuff

Tall Stuff

a novel by

Norma West Linder

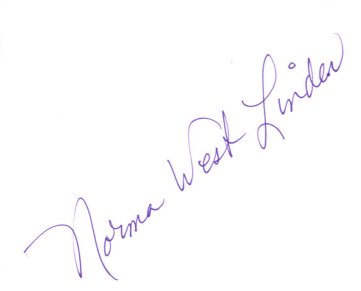

First Edition

Hidden Brook Press
www.HiddenBrookPress.com
writers@HiddenBrookPress.com

Copyright © 2016 Hidden Brook Press
Copyright © 2016 Norma West Linder

All rights for story and characters revert to the author. All rights for book, layout and design remain with Hidden Brook Press. No part of this book may be reproduced except by a reviewer who may quote brief passages in a review. The use of any part of this publication reproduced, transmitted in any form or by any means, electronic, mechanical, photocopied, recorded or otherwise stored in a retrieval system without prior written consent of the publisher is an infringement of the copyright law.

This book is a work of fiction. Names, characters, places and events are either products of the author's imagination or are employed fictitiously. Any resemblance to actual events, locales or persons, living or dead, is entirely coincidental.

Tall Stuff
by Norma West Linder

Cover Design – Richard M. Grove
Layout and Design – Richard M. Grove
Author Photograph – Grant Hill

Typeset in Garamond
Printed and bound in USA
Distributed in USA by Ingram
      in Canada by Hidden Brook Distribution

Library and Archives Canada Cataloguing in Publication

Linder, Norma West, 1928-, author
    Tall stuff / Norma West Linder.

ISBN 978-1-927725-38-2 (paperback)

    I. Title.

PS8573.I53T35 2016   C813'.54   C2016-904030-5

For James Edward Deahl
and all
Lovers of Live Theatre.

Table of Content

1 – Lust at First Sight – *p. 1*
2 – Mary Alice Has Her Ways – *p. 10*
3 – Motorcycle Madness – *p. 19*
4 – The Play's the Thing – *p. 26*
5 – Hot and Cold Stage Kisses – *p. 32*
6 – Scene in the Sinners Cellar – *p. 36*
7 – Surprise in a Pink Note – *p. 41*
8 – Victoria Speaks Up for Mitch – *p. 44*
9 – No Laughing Matter – *p. 50*
10 – Guess Who's Calling? – *p. 54*
11 – Max Greer's Heart to Heart With Tori – *p. 58*
12 – Good Advice from a Good Friend – *p. 62*
13 – Beside a Field of Buttercups – *p. 65*
14 – A Phone Call Cut Short – *p. 71*
15 – What is This Thing Called Love? – *p. 74*
16 – A Redheaded Stranger Appears – *p. 78*
17 – Definitely Not a Magnificent Obsession – *p. 82*
18 – Max Hosts an Afternoon Party – *p. 87*
19 – My Place or Yours? – *p. 92*
20 – Standard Dress Rehearsal – *p. 95*
21 – Tell Me Something I Don't Know – *p. 100*
22 – Town Talk Review of the Sunfield Players – *p. 105*
23 – Reaching a Final Decision – *p. 109*
24 – A Standing Ovation – *p. 112*
25 – Bella's Closing Night Party – *p. 115*
26 – Regret For What Might Have Been – *p. 124*
27 – Showdown Time – *p. 126*
28 – Tori Tells All to Millie – *p. 132*
29 – In The Doldrums of Bad Dreams – *p. 135*

30 – The Walking Wounded in Emergency – *p. 137*

31 – It's Not Always a Sin to Tell a Lie – *p. 140*

32 – Sometimes a Great Notion Comes in Red and Green – *p. 144*

33 – Victoria Meets Tuxedo the Cat – *p. 148*

34 – Jingle Bells and Wedding Bells – *p. 153*

35 – Valentines, Roses, and Raging Snowstorms – *p. 157*

Author Bio Note – *p. 162*

1

Lust at First Sight

BY THE TIME TORI WALKER TURNED TWELVE, she knew she was doomed to tower over her peers, and that awareness disturbed her. In Grade Seven, she felt like a giant among pygmies. Willing herself to stop growing didn't seem to help. Nothing helped.

"Bad weeds grow fast," her petite blonde mother would tease. "I should never have fed you so much spinach, so many vitamins when you were a baby."

Tori took after her father, a dark-haired six foot tall man with a ready smile and a way of making her feel better about her height. "You could be a fashion model," he'd suggest. "You have the right bone structure—high cheekbones and all. Even as a baby you were photogenic."

But Victoria had no desire to pursue a life under the bright lights of the modeling world. She'd found a toy nurse's set under the Christmas tree when she was five years old. From the time she'd unwrapped it and bandaged her first doll her only wish was to become a real nurse. Her brother Billy had changed his mind a dozen times about his goals in life, but Tori had remained steadfast. Perhaps losing her mother to cancer when Tori was only fourteen had something to do with it. Her sister Rita had been eighteen at the time and living with her boyfriend in her own little world. But Billy had been just ten years old, and Victoria had done her best to console him. Even though he didn't get in touch with her as often as she would have wished, she still felt a special affinity for him. It must have been comforting in old days, she reflected, when families stayed geographically close to each other. It wasn't easy maintaining long-distance relationships. She'd visited her dad often before his second wife

Tall Stuff

Nora had talked him into moving to the East Coast so she could be near her own people. Tori didn't blame her for that. Her dad was happy there—that was the way it should be. Women's Lib. *Wither thou goest I shall go* worked both ways. Her stepmother seemed to be trying to compensate by finding Tori a match, but so far she'd been spectacularly unsuccessful in those endeavours.

Now, at the age of twenty-seven, Victoria, all five feet, eleven and one-half inches of her—179 centimeters according to her driver's license, was employed as a registered nurse. Her first dream had come true, but the second one, a fervent wish to meet Mr. Right, had not. Some girls were content to settle for 'Mr. Right now', but she wasn't one of them. Tori had old-fashioned values. She wanted a future with a Golden Anniversary celebration in it. But the years were passing, and her dream man had not materialized. She thought her height was to blame. Men seemed to prefer petite women, women who made them feel big and powerful by comparison. Yet when she wasn't wearing her sensible white work shoes, Tori delighted in slipping into high heels, the higher the better. She had a red pair she was particularly fond of, even though they put her well over the six-foot mark.

As Victoria unlocked the door of the large apartment she shared with Mary Alice, a short man passed by, giving her a huge, flirty grin. She smiled, remembering an amusing scene from her teenage years. She'd been looking in the window of a jewelry store when she heard a voice behind her, a man's deep voice with a strong Latin accent. "You see something you like, tall stuff? I buy for you."

She'd turned to see a small, swarthy guy who couldn't have been more than five feet tall at the most. She'd walked away giggling without another backward glance.

Tori was still tickled by the memory as she unlaced and kicked off her white Keds. Other memories were not so pleasant, childhood memories of being relentlessly teased. "Tori Walker, ten-storey stilt walker!" was the most popular chant in elementary school. By the time she reached high school, she had the protection of a circle of friends, but sometimes even they teased her after she told them about the incident at the jewelry store. Her nickname became "Tall Stuff". The high school boys she might have had crushes on were invariably too short to be interested in her. Not that she found any of them particularly attractive, for that matter. She wanted a handsome guy she could look at eye to eye while standing up.

The telephone on the end table beside her easy chair broke into her thoughts with its demanding ring.

"Victoria?" Her stepmother's voice sounded breathless with excitement as she went on without waiting for a response. "There's someone you must meet. My friend Edie has this unmarried cousin who's an elementary teacher and he lives in your part of the country. She claims he'd be perfect for you. He's six feet tall and very interested in meeting someone."

"Nora, I'm much too busy these days," Tori lied. I'm perfectly content with my life the way it is."

"You'll change your tune one of these days. You'll meet that certain man and zap—it'll be love at first sight. You mark my words, it will happen when you least expect it."

What a laugh, Tori thought as she said her good-byes and replaced the receiver. Love at first sight. Ridiculous. Juvenile romanticism.

A week later, it happened. Mitch Ames moved into the vacant apartment across the hallway five doors away from her own. Well, maybe not love at first sight, but certainly lust. She almost ran into him with her laundry basket on her way to the elevator. He tossed her a careless "hi" and she'd felt her heart beat faster. Best of all, his chocolate-brown eyes looked directly into hers. She was still reeling from the feeling when she reached the laundry room in the basement of the building. Crazy as it seemed, she felt certain it had something to do with his smile—with the noticeable space between his front teeth. A sign of a generous nature, she'd once read. But his smile wasn't the only thing he had going for him. In the looks department, he had everything—thick chestnut hair sun bleached with highlights, big brown eyes, and a lean athletic body.

But he was obviously unimpressed by her, for the next time she passed him in the hallway he strode on by without acknowledging her presence. Perhaps he was just preoccupied, she thought, moving to a new apartment and all. But the rebuff brought back a painful childhood memory of a boy she'd had a major crush on. She still remembered his name. Joey Jackson. She'd fallen for him in a big way when she was in Grade Seven and he was one grade ahead of her. Her heart would beat faster each time she passed him in the hallway. Although she wanted to impress him, she was always struck dumb in his presence, too shy even to say hi. It still hurt, the memory of Joey Jackson. They'd gone to the same birthday party, a girl in her class who was turning thirteen. While the parents watched television in the living room above them, the young people in the rec room in the basement started a kissing game. It was called Spin the Bottle or something like that. One of the kids had learned about it from her grandmother, and she initiated it. The girls would sit in a circle on the floor and boys would take turns spinning a Coke bottle in the middle. He had to kiss whatever girl it pointed to when it stopped. Each time a boy and girl went behind the bathroom door to kiss, the others cheered them on. Tori's only recollection of the game was how thrilled she was when Joey turned out to be the one for her. Then he ruined it by shouting, "I'm not kissing ten-storey Tori. No way!"

She'd left the party in tears. When she got home, her mother was in the kitchen making chocolate chip cookies. She gave Tori a hug and sat her down at the table with a glass of cold milk and two cookies, still warm from the oven. No words were said. No words needed to be said.

Tori glanced down abashed at her wilted green uniform and scuffed shoes. After years on the maternity floor feeling envious of all the new mothers, she felt her transfer to Emergency couldn't come too soon. Being around babies made her yearn to hold one of her own. She even had names picked out, Zoe for a girl and Zak for a boy. But first she had to find a soul mate. Digging into her purse, she took out her key and let herself into her apartment.

Mary Alice was nestled in one end of their white velour sofa, painting the toenails of her left foot with a garish green enamel. It stank. Tori was about to remind her that she had her own bedroom for such purposes, but knowing it was useless, she simply collapsed in the nearest chair and picked up the daily paper featuring her favorite columnist, Andrew Macdonald. Reading his columns was one of her small pleasures in life—one she never tired of because he was always interesting.

"Have you met him yet?" her roommate asked without looking up.

"Met who?" Tori asked, well aware the girl was referring to the big handsome "who" down the hall from them.

"Mitch Ames. Our new neighbor." Mary Alice stretched one delicate foot under the critical gaze of her baby-blue eyes and continued. "He's twenty-eight years old and he's a bachelor. He's a chemical engineer with Lakeside Industries and he was transferred here from Edmonton. His hobbies are motorcycle racing, tennis, and community theatre. In that order."

"How in the world did you find out so much about him already? Sunfield isn't that small."

Mary Alice tightened the lid on her bottle of polish. "I have my ways," she replied smugly.

Tori decided to disappoint her by dropping the subject. She returned her attention to the *Town Talk* column. Andrew, she thought of him by his first name even though they hadn't met, was railing about the lack of manners in our present society. She found herself, as usual, agreeing with him. People didn't bother introducing friends when they stopped in public to chat with them. Clerks carried on personal telephone conversations while customers waited. The words *please* and *thank you* were in short supply. As one of her old teachers used to say, those words kept the machinery of life oiled and running free. "Listen to this, Mary Alice," urged Tori as she read the last of his column aloud.

'And while we're on the subject, I'm getting sick of the constant repetition of hearing everybody tell me that it's no problem to pour me more coffee, hold open a door, give me my change, or excuse me for calling the wrong number. Why can't people occasionally use that useful old phrase of you're welcome?'

Her roommate studied her. " So? What's your *problem*?" she asked, and Tori had to laugh in spite of herself.

"I'm getting hungry. Isn't it your turn to cook? I've had a busy day and I'm beat."

"I had a salad earlier, Tori. But maybe I could eat something else if you'll make it," Mary Alice added. "I know it was supposed to be my turn, but I feel kind of crampy."

In the kitchen, Tori found a sink full of dirty dishes and a messy table. Mary Alice could be exasperating, no doubt about it. Tori had formerly shared the place with the girl's older sister, but she had moved out of town. How could two sisters be so different? She grabbed an apron and started cleaning up the mess. Mary Alice used her period to stay home from work for two days every month, and she also used it for getting out of doing any work around the apartment. Tori was becoming more and more fed up with the unfair distribution of labor.

But her thoughts soon moved from her roommate's shortcomings to the wealth of information she'd provided about Mitch Ames. Mitch. The name suited him. He was certainly all male. Beautifully male. Those dark, deep-set eyes. How could she hope to attract him though? She began arranging her assets on one side of an imaginary ledger. She was quite intelligent. Of course, intelligence wasn't of prime importance when it came to attracting a man. Everyone said she had lovely hair, so black they thought at first she dyed it. A generous mouth and wide hazel eyes. Eyes that looked green whenever she wore that color. And she had a good sense of humor. On the debit side, she was too tall. Definitely too tall. "How's the weather up there?" jokesters used to ask. "Get nosebleeds often? I've lost my flagpole. Can I use you?" The lines were as endless as they were unfunny. But they hadn't made her slump—not physically anyway. Mitch was at least six feet tall, so maybe her height wouldn't matter to him. The trouble was her figure was more athletic than sexy. That *would* matter. And she didn't have Cinderella's feet. Her feet were too big. Size ten, sometimes even eleven. Tori remembered the words of an old Fats Waller song, words she'd learned by heart while living for a time with a jazz fan who considered Waller one of the true greats. "Mad at ya cause your feet's too big," she sang. "I really hate ya cause your feet's too big…" That romance had fizzled out because that boyfriend was more into music than he was into her. Figuratively and literally.

No doubt about it, the debit side of her personal ledger far outweighed the credit side. Her features were good but forgettable, and her voice held no trace of that sexy huskiness she so envied in others. Perhaps she could learn to cultivate one like Mary Alice's. She always managed a husky voice whenever there was a man within hearing range. When Tori tried it, her date would invariably ask if she was coming down with a cold.

The dishes finished, she made herself a cheese sandwich, buttered it on the outside, and waited for it to brown in the electric frying pan. Watching it sizzle, she tried to keep from thinking about the tasty gourmet meals she had shared with Mary Alice's sister. It wasn't too difficult. Food was the last thing on her mind. Her thoughts kept returning to Mitch Ames like pigeons coming home to roost. She simply had to get to know him. But how? Perhaps it could be something small—something like dropping her door key as he passed by. No. That would only make her look clumsy. Maybe struggling under the weight of too many bags of groceries. No. Too obvious. She'd feel like a fool. And look like one too. But there had to be some way to do it. He was the most attractive man she'd ever laid eyes on. And he was taller than she was by a good two inches.

As Tori conjured up and abandoned new strategies, Mary Alice came into the kitchen, moving quietly in her fuzzy pink slippers. "Something sure smells good," she said, hugging her flowered housecoat tightly around her. "I'm still hungry after all."

She flopped down on one of their red leather stools by the counter.

"There's more cheese in the fridge," said Tori.

"Then you won't mind if I have this one. You're a darling, Tori, you really are."

Victoria made no reply as she grimly set about making another sandwich.

"Why don't we ask him over for a drink? Tell him welcome to our building."

The question caught Tori off guard, and her face lit up before she could even think of concealing her pleasure at the suggestion. Mary Alice should start a detective agency. She'd make a fortune. "Ask who?" she demanded, fooling nobody.

"The new tenant, of course. You've been mooning over him ever since you came in. I could tell by the look on your face."

Good God, the girl was a witch. She should be grilled along with the sandwich. Still, the idea had merit. The straightforward approach. It might just work.

"You ask him," said Tori.

"Me? Why me?"

"Because it was your idea."

Such warped logic always worked with Mary Alice and this was no exception. "I'll do it after you make us a pot of coffee and another sandwich," she agreed.

Tori's heart started doing time and a half though she chided herself for behaving like a schoolgirl. She could scarcely wait to put the plan into action. She'd wear her new blue silk blouse, she decided. And her bright golden hoop earrings.

Tall Stuff

Casually handsome in a grey cashmere sweater and tight black jeans, Mitch Ames had arrived at exactly seven minutes after eight by Tori's watch. It was now nearly nine o'clock, and his attention was still riveted exclusively on Mary Alice Mathews. Tori could have strangled her. The younger girl had changed into a pink angora sweater and matching pants and, as usual, she wore no bra. According to the rule, Tori knew, you were supposed to wear one if you could hold a pencil beneath one of your breasts without letting it fall. Hell, her roommate could hold a flashlight there with no trouble. But Tori had to admit she looked great. Roundly firm and firmly round, damn her anyway.

Mary Alice trained her ingenuous blue eyes on Tori. "Do we have any crackers left?" she asked. "And some of that old cheddar would be good with this wine."

Good for a small blonde rat, Tori fumed as she stalked out to the kitchen. The music from their living room was just loud enough to keep her from hearing what was being said as she prepared a plate of celery stalks, cheese, olives and crackers for nibbling. It was sweet, bubbly music—the kind Tori loathed as much as Mary Alice liked it. The kind of music that made her want to fling the disc out the nearest window.

When she rinsed her hands under the cold water tap, Tori accidentally splashed the front of her blue blouse. She cursed softly, then shrugged. Mitch hadn't noticed it dry, why would he notice it wet? Maybe she should walk back in there soaking wet. Like some gal in a wet tee shirt contest. It might be one way of getting him to actually see her. Maybe she should walk in backwards…

For an uncomfortable moment, Tori stopped and tried to take stock of herself. How could she let this happen to her? How could she allow herself to behave this way? She wasn't sixteen years old. For years, she'd prided herself on being cool and self-possessed. What she felt for Mitch, she reasoned, was nothing more than an extra strong chemical reaction. Ignore it long enough and it would go away. The trouble was, though, she couldn't ignore it at all. The mere presence of him in their apartment had her heart doing flip flops.

Slowly, Tori became aware that the sound of voices had ceased. Plate in hand, she hurried back into the living room.

Mary Alice was dancing to the frothy music, pirouetting gracefully as she circled the room. Her eyes were closed and she was wearing a dreamy expression. But she was dancing alone.

Tori was stunned. "Where is he?" she asked when she finally found her voice.

"Where's…"

"Mary Alice, if you say 'Where's who?' I'll dump this plate of goodies over your head. Dammit, I swear I will."

The younger girl opened her eyes. "He's gone," she said

"Gone without even saying good-night to me? What a boor! Andrew Macdonald was certainly spot on about the lack of good manners today."

"Tori, you're always quoting that Macdonald guy. My dad would have called him an old curmudgeon."

"Andrew's not old, not according to his picture. Anyway, never mind all that. Just tell me what happened."

"He asked me out, I said nothing doing, and he took off."

"You said *no*?"

"You got it."

"But why? My god, he's a real hunk!"

Mary Alice took a piece of cheese and studied it as though it might contain the answer.

"Why did you refuse him?" Tori went on. "How *could* you refuse him?"

"I don't know exactly. It's just that there's something…I don't know…something almost scary about him. Anyway what difference does it make to you whether I go out with Mitch Ames or not. You're the one with the hots for him—not me."

Tori winced at the hated expression. But she couldn't deny the truth of the words. And she couldn't tell Mary Alice that seeing him call for her would have been better than not seeing him at all. He'd soon see that the girl was an airhead, and then she'd have a chance to win him over. Now she'd have to think of another way to do it. Tori felt certain she'd stand a good chance if only they could get to know each other. Scary, Mary Alice called him. What a silly idea. Why would anyone be frightened of Mitch Ames?

2
Mary Alice Has Her Ways

As late summer ripened into fall, Tori fought a losing battle to remain aloof whenever she passed Mitch Ames in the hallway. Each time he greeted her, the deep timbre of his voice filled her with wistful longing. He didn't always say hello; sometimes he appeared lost in thought, and she was certain he was looking right through her. When he did favor her with his special smile, her bones turned to water and she could think of nothing else for hours.

If this is love, she mused, it's something to be devoutly avoided. Almost like a sickness. She had taken to brushing her black, blunt-cut hair till it sent off sparks and spending hours as well as dollars on her make-up. All to no avail. Other men asked her out, but she refused all offers. She'd had enough of casual dating. It was Mitch or no one for her. And she knew that this time she wanted everything up to and including the house in the suburbs and a couple of kids. There was no point in telling herself to be reasonable. She had gone beyond reason. She was fed up with all her so-called freedom. She wanted to be tied to a husband, home and family. And she wanted it now—or at least as soon as possible. Most of all, she wanted it with Mitch. She'd never before felt such a strong attachment for any man.

Tori was feeling particularly restless when she returned from the hospital on a Friday evening early in September. With a jaundiced eye, she watched Mary Alice preparing for a date. How could Mitch have preferred her? Couldn't he see the girl was all wrong for him? Everything about her was so obvious—the frankly fake platinum hair, the roundly curled eyelashes, the pink cupid's bow painted carefully above her own thin upper lip. Still, Tori had to admit Mary Alice was cute in a baby doll sort of way. Her figure was enticingly curvacious. She knew how to dress. And she was seven years Tori's junior.

"Who's the lucky guy tonight?" she asked.

"Somebody I met online," Mary Alice replied. "I knew if I went fishing often enough I'd catch one worth keeping. You should try it. There are plenty of fish in the sea, believe me."

"What's this fish do for a living?"

"He's a jockey. Don't you dare laugh when you see him. He's really a sweet guy."

"Why should I laugh?"

"Because he's a tiny guy about five feet tall. And he has the brightest red hair you ever saw. Almost orange."

"I'd better be sure to be sitting down when he gets here. Else the two of us will look like a flaming match beside a telephone pole."

Mary Alice giggled. "I'm even taller than him. By two or three inches. I'd better wear flats."

"He'll probably grip you between his legs when he kisses you."

"Don't be gross," Mary Alice retorted. But she was still giggling when the doorbell rang.

The apartment became oppressively quiet after Mary Alice left with her jockey. Tori wandered out to the kitchen to make a cup of coffee. She was drinking too much of it, she told herself, both at the hospital and at home. But it gave her something to do. She thought about watching television but rejected the idea. She knew she'd be looking at some sit com and thinking about Mitch. She wondered where he was tonight. She hadn't run into him in the hallway for several days now, and she missed even those brief encounters. The lyrics of an old number came to her. "I've got it bad, and that ain't good", she sang out. Never get involved with a music buff, she told herself. Lines and phrases to fit every situation keep coming back—like a song.

As she sipped black coffee at the kitchen counter, Tori reached for the newspaper. She paused when she came to Andrew Macdonald's *Town Talk* column. His picture showed a serious looking blond man. Tonight's offering was all about community theatre. Apparently they were about to cast the first play of the season, a comedy called *Banana Boats at Midnight*. Something clicked in Tori's mind. "That's it!" she shouted, tossing the paper aside. Mary Alice had mentioned that theatre was one of Mitch's hobbies the very first time they'd talked about him. He'd surely be at the first reading of the year. Her mind raced. Who did she know in the group? There must be somebody. Of course. Allen Saunders. She'd noticed his name in the program in the last play she'd gone to see. But that was a couple of years ago. Still, it might be worth a try. She and Allen had attended the same high school. He'd had a crush on her, but he was heavily into the drama group and she wasn't, so nothing ever came of it.

She looked up his number in the phone book and dialed it. He answered on the fourth ring, just as she was about to give up.

"This is Victoria Carter, Allen. Do you remember me? We went to high school together."

She paused, giving him time to place her, but he answered almost at once. "Tori! Of course I remember you. How are you? "

"Restless," she replied. "This may come as a shock, but how do I go about getting into the community theatre scene? I need some sort of diversion from my work at the hospital."

He hesitated, but not for long. "It's easy, Tori. We'd be glad to have you. We're holding readings next Thursday. Why don't you come and try out?"

She faltered, at once frightened and intrigued by the idea. "I was just thinking...something backstage maybe." If only she could land a part, she thought, and play it well. What better way to impress Mitch?

"Read first," he said. "We could do with some new faces onstage—especially one as pretty as yours."

"Still the gallant Allen. What's the play about?"

"It's a comedy called *Banana Boats at Midnight*. It's pretty raunchy. It might shock the local burghers out of their seats but it should be lots of fun. I'm thinking of reading for it. You should too."

"You did say *burghers*, didn't you?"

He chuckled "I see you still have a weird sense of humor. I'll pick you up on Thursday if you like."

"I would like. Moral support and all that."

"Good. It's a date then. I'll call for you at a quarter to eight. Can't wait to see you again, Tall Stuff. Hey—sorry—that just slipped out"

"No worry. Thanks, Allen. Apartment twenty-two, three- forty Riverside Avenue. I'll be ready."

Tori felt a twinge of guilt as she replaced the receiver. Allen had sounded so excited about the prospect of seeing her again. But wasn't any tactic fair in love and war?

The next few days flew by in a heady wave of anticipation. Though she'd never done any acting, it didn't look all that difficult to her. She hoped her height wouldn't put her at a disadvantage. If Mitch were to play the leading man, they'd be perfect together.

Allen Saunders rang her bell promptly at seven forty-five on Thursday evening. He still looked like the gangly youth she remembered. His khaki pants were baggy at the knees and his white sweatshirt was streaked with green paint. His hair was still the color of beach sand after a heavy rain, and he wore the thick glasses she recalled all too well.

"Let's go," she said. "Are you sure you don't mind driving me?"

"A pleasure," he replied. Before he let her into his maroon Chevy sedan, he grabbed a cloth from the dashboard and wiped off the seat.

"You'll spoil me," Tori protested, but she found the small gesture oddly appealing.

Before they'd been in the community theatre building five minutes, Tori was painfully aware of being overdressed. All the people there, young and old, were wearing tee shirts and jeans. Hoping no one would notice, she removed her dangling gold earrings and stuffed them into her purse. But she could do nothing about the clingy silk tangerine pantsuit she'd chosen for the occasion. She began to read the clippings plastered on a bulletin board about the previous season's plays, but Allen took her arm and insisted on leading her away on a grand tour of the place.

The building was old but well kept. As they prowled the area backstage, a slightly musty odor assailed her nostrils which, strangely, was not altogether unpleasant. It seemed charged with the distilled excitement of a hundred past plays. As she strolled with Allen out to the centre of the stage, more people began to arrive. Some of them were throwing open the windows that lined one side of the auditorium. A light breeze ruffled the worn blue curtains like the ghosts of dramas yet to come.

Tori stared out at the rows of empty seats. "It's quite a building, Allen."

Tall Stuff

"We're pretty proud of it, such as it is. At least it's our own. We do all our rehearsals here except for the final dress rehearsal. For that we move to the downtown theatre."

"Do you get many new members each season?" She tried to make the question sound casual, but she was getting concerned. She hadn't as yet seen any sign of Mitch.

"Some come—some leave," he replied. "But we usually have about fifty members." He glanced at his watch. "We'd better get up to the greenroom. It's about time to start the readings. I think I'll get brave and try out for a role this time. I'm tired of always working backstage."

The went through a side door of the auditorium into a long, narrow workroom half filled with dusty flats and discarded props and started up a sharply angled stairway. She followed him along a hallway into a large apple-green room edged with a thin grey line of metal chairs, broken here and there by ancient horsehair sofas and armchairs.

"This greenroom really is green," she quipped.

"Shh!" someone hissed, and Tori felt the color rise to her cheeks.

Like a king on his throne, Max Greer, lean, angular and intense, was seated at the far end of the room in front of a moss-colored card table as a dozen people leafed through copies of the play. Tori noted with dismay that Mitch Ames was not among them. She and Allen tip-toed across the varnished floor and sat facing the open doorway. She studied her hands as several throat-clearing sounds punctuated the silence.

Max Greer rose to welcome everyone and give them a brief run-down of the play. "We'll start at page twenty-three," he announced. "Scene Two."

Tori found the page and tried to keep her mind on it as two late-coming women mumbled apologies and hurried in to take seats. Then all at once he stood framed in the doorway, more dashing than ever in a red sweat shirt and black jeans. His eyes widened in recognition when they met hers, and he hurried over to take the empty seat beside her. "Hello," he whispered. "I didn't know you'd be here."

Tori decided to refrain from mentioning that she was a brand new recruit. She turned to Allen and made hasty introductions before Max rapped loudly for silence.

Since the script called for three men and eight women, several people were asked to read before the director turned to Tori.

"You read Priss this time," he ordered. "Allen, you take the boyfriend, and the fellow there in the red sweater, would you be the Professor? Start at Scene Three on page thirty-six."

Tori glanced quickly down the page. She didn't come in till the bottom of thirty-eight. Her heart was hammering so outrageously she was certain everyone could hear it. But she mustn't muff her big chance. She had to get the part. For Mitch. He was delivering his lines in a deep, sure baritone. He was certain to be cast, she thought.

After a few breathless seconds, the heavy lettering of PRISS wavered before her frightened eyes. She began to read in a tremulous soprano, the book shaking so she could barely hold it. She moved it from one hand to the other and finally brought it to rest on her knees, determination steadying her voice, but only a little.

During one of Priss' longer speeches, Tori became aware of a strange snorting sound to her far left. Someone was laughing at her! Her face began to burn with humiliation, and as soon as the scene was over she ran from the room. She was halfway down the stairs before Allen caught up with her.

"What's wrong?" he asked.

"Oh, Allen, I know I wasn't that good, but how could anybody be so rude! Somebody was laughing at me."

"What are you talking about?"

"Someone was snickering. I heard them."

For a few seconds, Allen looked perplexed. Then he grinned. "You heard Jerry," he explained. "Our lighting man. He has a nasal obstruction of some kind and has to clear his head like that now and then. We're all so used to it we don't even hear it any more." He squeezed her arm. "Come on back now, and stop being so silly. You were doing a terrific job."

"Allen, I can't go back. I'd look a fool."

"No, you wouldn't. Nobody will pay any attention. It's par for the course. People are always going off on emotional tangents around here. Come on."

For some reason, Tori found herself more relaxed than before when she apologized and Max asked her to resume reading the part of Priss. The time flew by, and at ten o'clock they broke for coffee. Max remained alone at his card table, thoughtfully chewing his pencil and running his fingers through his dark curly hair. The air was charged with suspense.

Tori made a cursory exploration of the costume and make-up rooms before returning to the kitchenette. A WORSH YER MUG sign above the sink brought a smile to her lips. She rinsed out Allen's mug as well as her own. Would she get the part? She thought she'd read pretty well—she and Allen and Mitch worked easily and naturally together. But the woman called Gloria something or other—the one with a voluptuous build had done a pretty good characterization of Priss too.

"Have you noticed an odd thing about this play?" Allen asked as they were returning to their seats.

"What's that?" Tori mumbled absently. Mitch seemed to be paying a lot of attention to her rival for the role of Priss. She had to admit Gloria was attractive with her big brown eyes and wealth of auburn hair that looked to be straight out of a shampoo commercial.

"You didn't even hear my question, did you?"

"No," she confessed, weak with relief as Mitch returned to sit beside her once more. "Sorry, Allen. I was daydreaming."

"I was just asking if you noticed this play has nothing whatsoever to do with banana boats."

"So why the title?"

"I suppose it's an attention grabber. Norman Mailer did the same with one of his novels. I think he called it *Why are We in Viet Nam?* But it wasn't about the war at all. At the end, the son was going off to Viet Nam, but that's all I remember about it. It was published years and years ago. Mailer was a big name at one time."

"Never heard of him. Or his novels. You always were a bookworm, Allen. Not much wonder you ended up owning a bookstore."

"Thanks to a legacy from my grandfather. It's a great little store. One you've never entered, much to my regret. Guess you're not much of a reader."

"I do have a library card," she retorted.

"And just how does that help us little independent bookstores, pray tell?"

Max Greer rapped resoundingly for silence and the buzz of conversation ceased.

The last part of the reading went well, but to Tori's disappointment, Gloria was asked to read Priss again after only a few pages. Max seemed to be having trouble making up his mind. It was past eleven-thirty when the auditions finally broke up. "We'll have to finish casting tomorrow night," the director informed them. "I'm undecided about some of the parts. You—the new fellow in the red sweater. You read very well. Will you take on the Professor?"

Mitch leaned back and folded his arms. "Will do," he replied. "Sounds like fun."

"And you, Allen. Let's have you out there in front of the footlights for a change. The boyfriend. Okay?"

"Okay," agreed Allen, looking immensely pleased.

Max closed his book. "That's it then, kiddies," he said. "Keep your copies of the play and I'll see you tomorrow night." He threw all his papers into a briefcase and was first out the door.

Tori covered her disappointment by congratulating Mitch and Allen. "What time will he want us tomorrow?" she asked.

"Seven-thirty," said Allen. "I can pick you up if you like."

She stared at Mitch and as though on cue he said, "Tori and I live in the same building. She might as well come with me. Matter of fact, I can drive her home tonight. You don't mind, do you, kid?"

"Matter of fact, I do mind. But I guess it's up to Tori."

Feeling Allen's eyes staring at her from behind their thick lenses, Tori wrestled briefly with her conscience. Her conscience won. "Give me a rain check till tomorrow night, Mitch. We'll come together then."

All the way down the steep stairway, she was mentally kicking herself. What a fool she was! Passing up her first chance to be alone with Mitch. She must be out of her mind. He was probably chatting up her buxom rival for the part right now—the part of his girlfriend. The part she longed for.

Allen got her coat from the front hall and they left the building.

Although she tried hard to attentive to Allen on the way home, her thoughts were all centered on Mitch. To compensate, she invited him in for coffee, glad for once that Mary Alice would monopolize the conversation. Her roommate lost no time in doing so. Mary Alice could talk the legs off a table. There were never any awkward silences when she was around. Tori sensed that Allen was hoping to have some time alone with her, but she knew that wasn't going to happen.

Before he left, Allen turned to her. "If you get the part," he said, "and I hope you do, you'll have to show up for every rehearsal. How are you going manage that when you're working?"

"No problem, Allen. I've already arranged for a two-month leave of absence from the hospital. I need a break. These twelve-hour shifts have worn me to a frazzle. I've been working steadily since I graduated and I need a bit of R and R. They were very understanding about it."

"Speaking of R and R, you won't find being involved in community theatre very restful or relaxing, Tori. Max Greer can be one tough taskmaster. He's the best director we have, but he can be brutal."

She smiled. "I'll survive. They say a change is as good as a rest. But thanks for the warning."

If she got the part of Priss, Tori reflected before she fell asleep, she and Mitch Ames would be seeing a lot of each other. She had to get the role. She absolutely *had* to!

3

Motorcycle Madness

MITCH KNOCKED ON HER DOOR at ten minutes past seven the next evening. He greeted her briefly before looking around. "Where's your roommate?" he asked.

"Probably out with her latest boyfriend. She sent her jockey riding off into the sunset, but I have a hunch this new love of hers might be serious. She's very secretive about him, and that's not like her."

Tori thought she saw a look of disappointment flit across his handsome face. She hoped it was just her imagination working overtime. "Let's go," she said. "I'm all set. I really want to get that part."

"I think you have a good chance. You read it well."

"Think there might be a casting couch?" she joked. "I really want that part."

Mitch grinned at her and she noted with satisfaction that he had to look down because she was wearing jeans and sneakers. His size made her feel almost delicate, and it was a good sensation, one she seldom experienced.

"You feeling brave?" he asked as they left the building.

"Why do you ask?"

"It's a nice evening. We could take my chopper instead of the car. Better button up your jacket, though. It's a bit windy."

Tori swallowed hard. She'd always been nervous around motorcycles. She'd seen too many mangled bodies because of them. It seemed every few months cyclists were being admitted to Emergency. Too often, they were beyond help.

"Come on, be a sport. You only live once."

That's what's holding me back, she thought. But he was smiling down at her and she was possessed by an overpowering urge to please him. It dawned on her she'd be hugging him all the way to the community theatre building if they cycled there. That settled the matter. "Just promise me you won't go too fast," she said. "Especially around the corners. I get nervous just thinking about them."

The thrill of hugging Mitch disappeared with the first turn. She felt as though her right leg was about to make contact with pavement at any moment. He was deliberately trying to frighten her, she thought, and she almost hated him for it. "Hey—take it easy," she hollered, but her words were lost in the rush of wind.

After what seemed an endless ride, he came to a stop in front of the building. Tori was trembling as she dismounted from the big red Harley, too shaken even to reach up and remove her shiny black helmet. "You did that on purpose!" she accused.

"Did what?"

"You know damn well what. You drove like a maniac because you knew I was nervous."

He chuckled. "Had to get you here on time, didn't I? I'll take it easy going home."

"I'm taking a cab home. Or I'll ask Allen."

"Oh, come on, Tori, don't be like that." He reached for her hand and she felt herself weakening as he went on. "I'm sorry if I frightened you. Really I am. Most girls like to ride fast. I thought you were just kidding about being nervous. Now that I know it bothers you, I won't do it again. Honestly. Am I forgiven?"

Lost in the wonder of his face so close to hers, Tori could only nod.

"Good. Now let's go in there so you can walk off with the part of Priss. Bring your helmet with you. Sometimes people nick them."

Tori found herself wishing she shared his confidence in her acting ability. She wanted the role so much she was afraid her desperation would show through and she'd lose out. Stay cool, she told herself. Hang loose. She took several deep breaths on the way up the stairs and was reasonably collected by the time she and Mitch sat down and the final reading began.

A collective sigh of relief went up a couple of hours later when Max announced it was time for a coffee break. Everyone began milling around. In the small kitchen, Gloria continued an animated conversation with Tori. "Just imagine," she was saying. "People are always asking me how I get roped into taking parts in these plays. *Roped into* indeed! They have no idea how we fight tooth and claw for the privilege. I've even seen women weep when they miss out on parts they had their hearts set on."

I might be one of them, Tori mused, as she muttered something non-committal in reply. Gloria had a strange accent—one that was hard to place. Behind them, another female was sounding off. "I'll be thrilled even if I only get the part of the maid. I know I could make something out of that role, something the audience would remember. I could do a curtain call with the rose between my teeth."

"There are no small parts," a male voice boomed. "Only small actors."

How vulnerable these people are, Tori thought. Of all the community theatre plays she'd seen, she'd never been able to remember who played what two weeks later. For that matter, she couldn't even recall the names of the last Oscar winners.

"Didn't anyone make Max a coffee?" enquired a silver-haired man with a pronounced British accent.

"I'll do it, darling," said Gloria. "Anything to get on the good side of the director." She winked at Tori as she spoke, but Tori sensed beneath the playful manner she was deadly serious. They were rivals and they knew it.

The last part of the readings passed in a whirl of nervous excitement. Max announced his choices for the remainder of the cast, leaving the role of Priss till the very end. He looked from Tori to Gloria and back again. The silence was tense. He cleared his throat. "Now for the part of Priss," he said quietly.

Tori dug her fingernails into her palms.

"Victoria Walker."

He said the name slowly and for a second or two, Tori couldn't believe her ears. Her mind raced. Rehearsals wouldn't be a problem. She'd been granted her leave of absence, so she'd be free to study like mad to do justice to the role. Best of all, she'd be playing opposite Mitch. They could rehearse together. It was perfect. She couldn't help briefly wondering how Max Greer would react if he knew she was completely inexperienced in acting, but she pushed that thought far back in her mind. At least this play wasn't a Festival entry. In any case, she was far too happy to entertain any serious misgivings.

"Well, Victoria," said Max, favoring her with one of his rare smiles, "do you want the part or not?"

Tori found her voice. "I do," she replied, "I definitely do."

"That's it, then. We rehearse Mondays, Wednesdays, and Thursdays. Seven-thirty sharp. I want everyone here for the first one. And that means everyone. We have only six weeks. We have to make every one of those weeks count. Thanks, kiddies. See you Monday."

Allen was the first to grasp Tori's hand and congratulate her, but the others were quick to join him. They were almost child-like in their excitement. She felt a twinge of conscience. She hoped she wouldn't let them down. Gloria was the only one to keep a cool distance. She'd taken on the task of working on props for the play rather than being left out altogether. Tori couldn't help wondering if she had done so in order to be involved in the play or whether she too was interested in becoming involved with Mitch. She kept sending flirtatious glances his way. And she wasn't the only one. He was so incredibly good-looking there was bound to be lots of competition. But being overly possessive would be the surest way to kill any interest Mitch might have in her. She'd have to train herself to stay cool.

"Want to stop for a drink on the way home?" he asked as they started down the stairs. "We should celebrate."

"I'd like to have a couple of doubles before I get back on that mechanical monster of yours."

"I'll be careful, Tori, I promise. I'll drive as though I have a crate of eggs riding behind me."

"You'll turn my head with compliments like that," she retorted.

Since they were wearing jeans, they settled on the Sinners Cellar, a bistro not far from the theatre building. When they were seated at a corner table, an uncomfortable silence prevailed until the waitress came to take their order.

"Wadda ya want?" the girl asked, shifting her gum from one side of her jaw to the other.

Tori grinned at Mitch. "I'll have a rum and 7 Up," she said. "Light rum."

Hands on hips, the waitress turned to Mitch and repeated her question. "Scotch," he replied. "Haig and Haig. On the rocks."

Tori saw that he was having trouble keeping a straight face. She leaned forward when the girl left. "She's a real winner, isn't she?"

The waitress returned before there was time to reply. "We don't have no hag 'n hag," she said, looking even grouchier than before.

Mitch leaned back and exhaled. "Okay, just bring me the bar scotch."

Tori was glad the girl's behavior gave them something to make small talk about. Maybe years from now they'd still remember this, she thought, chiding herself in the next breath for being so hopelessly romantic.

When at last she brought their drinks, the waitress slammed them down so hard Tori feared the glasses would break. "Fourteen-thirty-five," she demanded.

Tori noticed that Mitch took pains to find and give her the exact amount. She dumped it on her tray and waited a few seconds, but when Mitch continued to ignore her she finally turned and left them.

"Good thing we only want one drink," said Tori. "I don't think she'll be back. I've never seen such a grim waitress."

Mitch took a sip of his drink, made a face, and set it down. "She must get good tips from masochists," he joked.

Tori agreed, and they finished their drinks in a silence that was a little more comfortable than before. As they were leaving, Tori caught the eye of a blonde man who sat hunched over a beer at one end of the bar. He looked oddly familiar, but gave no sign of recognition as they passed. Perhaps he had been a patient of hers. She didn't think so, though. But where had she seen him? The question continued to plague her as she and Mitch donned their glittering metallic helmets and mounted his cycle. But hugging him as they headed off in the cool night air soon erased such thoughts from her mind. She gloried in the nearness of his body, as, true to his word, he took it easy this time.

As he parked his Harley at the back of her apartment building, she screwed up her courage. "Want to come in for a nightcap? I think there's some Merlot left."

"Mind if I take a rain check on that, Tori. I'm really beat."

She tried hard to mask her disappointment. "No problem," she said thinking of how Andrew Macdonald would have scoffed at her reply.

Tall Stuff

Then Mitch surprised her by an abrupt change of heart. "Why not come to my place," he said. "I've got some good Jamaican rum you can sample."

"Sold," she replied.

"You were right—this is good," Tori said, sipping her drink and stretching out her long legs as she tried to get comfortable in one corner of his black leather sofa. She glanced around. He certainly kept the place spotless. It was like a magazine layout of the ideal bachelor's apartment. Good abstract art, red leather bar, white scatter rugs and all. He probably had a cleaning woman. Or a gullible girlfriend. She almost wished she was a smoker so she could dirty the big white marble ashtray beside her. Anything to make the place look lived in. There must be something between this perfection and Mary Alice's sloppiness. He'd put on a CD, and romantic violin music drifted around them from unseen speakers.

By the time she was finishing her drink and wearying of making all the small talk herself, Mitch had lowered both the lights and the music. Tori knew he was about to kiss her, so she set her glass down and turned towards him. His dark eyes held hers like a physical grip; she breathed his name as his mouth sought hers. She closed her eyes. His kisses were not gentle, but he brushed his lips against her neck, teasing her a little before each one. She was too smitten to stop him when he reached his hand under her tee shirt, but when he started working on her jeans, she sat up. "Let's not rush things, Mitch. I feel as though I scarcely know you…"

He pulled her close. "We're not rushing things, Tori. Things are rushing us. Come on. Don't shut me out."

"I'm not, Mitch. I just don't want to go too far too fast." She struggled out of his arms. "I guess I'm an old-fashioned girl at heart."

Looking sullen, he rose and straightened his hair and clothing. "You're free to go home with your virtue intact," he said. "I thought we were on the same wave-length. Obviously, I was mistaken."

"I'm sorry if I gave you the wrong impression. I wanted so much to…"

"Let's drop it, shall we?" He strode across the room and held the door open while she retrieved her jacket from the hall closet. "See you around, Tori."

Feeling as though she'd been punched in the stomach, Victoria walked past him and out into the hallway. His door was closed firmly behind her. She was furious with him for behaving so badly. But she was even more furious with herself because she knew, deep down inside, she still wanted him.

Though her vision was blinded by tears, Tori was surprised to see a retreating figure hurrying towards the elevator. She was certain it was Allen Saunders. What would he be doing here at this hour?

4
The Play's the Thing

TORI SPENT A SLEEPLESS FRIDAY NIGHT which led into a miserable weekend. Questions haunted her, questions for which she could find no reasonable answers. Would Mitch call for her Monday for rehearsal? Had she ruined everything between them with her foolish hesitation? What had Allen Saunders been doing in the hallway? Who was that familiar looking blonde man she'd seen in the Sinners Cellar? Questions and more questions. It was as though strange voices were constantly interrogating her. But the biggest question of all was whether she'd spoiled things between herself and Mitch.

Mary Alice was out most of the time. Tori heard someone call for her early Saturday evening but remained secluded in her room with the door shut, trying to read a novel but unable to keep her mind on its plot. She sometimes wished she could be as carefree as Mary Alice. Maybe she should have taken a business course instead of going into nursing. Then she wouldn't have needed this break. She, too, would have been a free spirit on weekends—after five days of less demanding work and easy hours. But an office routine had never appealed to her. Despite everything, she liked her work at the hospital. It was challenging, but always interesting. And she felt she was doing something important, something to help humanity. Even in her present despondent mood, she still believed that. She knew she'd be more than ready to go back when her leave of absence was up.

Even if Mitch didn't call for her Monday evening at least they'd be reading together at rehearsal. She would manage somehow to make him want her again. She'd been crazy to worry about his thinking she was too easy. After all, this was the twenty-first century and they weren't teenagers. She was tempted to pick up the phone and call him. He'd given her his number in the Sinners Cellar and she knew it by heart. Earlier, she's actually started to call it but had chickened out at the last minute, her heart pounding like mad. Phoning him might be the wrong move. She couldn't afford a second mistake.

Shortly after midnight, she gave up all pretense of reading. All she could think about, all she really wanted to think about was Mitch Ames. His dark eyes. His beautiful smile with the diastema. That's what the little space between his front teeth was called. It was supposed to be a sign of a generous nature she'd read somewhere. She'd tell him about that as soon as she had a chance. He was absolutely the sexiest man she'd ever seen. Tori finally fell asleep, pleasuring herself as she thought about his hot kisses.

On Sunday morning, she called her best friend Kate. "I need a friend to talk to," she said. "Will you be home this afternoon?"

"I'm always here for you. You know that. Anyway, it's about time you visited your godchild. It's been a couple of weeks."

"I know. I'm sorry. I have the cutest Beatrix Potter mug for her—one I found last time I was in Hallmark's."

"Tori, you don't have to bring her a present every time you come. Wait for her first birthday."

Kate had coffee and freshly baked cinnamon rolls ready when Victoria arrived. "You're just in time to put Dana down for her nap," she said.

Tori picked up the tired infant. "Mmm—she still has that lovely baby smell. You're so lucky, Kate. You have everything I want."

When they had the baby settled down with a bottle, Kate turned to her. "Okay, what's the rest of the story about this new man in your building and your doing a role in community theatre?"

"A leading role, actually, Kate. I play the part of Priss in a comedy and Priss is anything but prissy. I'm glad my dad and Nora live too far away to come to the opening. They'd be shocked by some of the language. Well, Nora would be anyway."

"Bob and I will come and see you."

"Kate, I know you don't much like community theatre."

"But I *do* like you. Now about this man?"

"I accused him of moving too fast, he got angry and I haven't heard from him since Friday night."

"Maybe he *was* moving too fast. Guys are easier to get than they are to get rid of sometimes. Are you sure he's right for you?"

"Absolutely. He's the proverbial tall, dark and handsome and I'm crazy about him. We've both been cast in this play."

"Then go for it, Tori. Get him back and let him reach for a Trojan next time you're together. Hey, remember that first boyfriend of yours? The one who told you he wanted to make sure you had an organism? They laughed, recalling their high school days together when everyone called them the long and short of it because Kate was so short and Tori so tall. The afternoon passed in shared girl talk, one memory triggering another until Kate's husband returned from his golf club.

Monday came and Tori had neither seen nor heard from Mitch. Early in the evening the doorbell rang and she rushed to answer it. She was surprised to see Allen Saunders standing there.

"Allen! What are you doing here?"

He flushed slightly and grinned. "Ringing your bell, for one thing."

He looked neater than she'd ever seen him. "Aren't you going to invite me in?" he asked as she continued to stare.

"Allen, I'm sorry. Of course, come in. Here—let me take your jacket."

As she hung the brown suede jacket in the hall closet, Tori searched her mind for some clue that would explain his presence. Had he said anything about picking her up for tonight's rehearsal? No, she would have remembered if they'd made any such plans. She wished Mary Alice would finish whatever she was doing and join them. It might be less uncomfortable with three of them to make conversation.

"Is your neighbor taking you to rehearsal tonight?" Allen asked.

"Mitch? No, I don't think so. I haven't seen him since Friday."

"Well why don't you come along with us? No point in both of us driving."

"Us?" Tori repeated, making no attempt to hide her confusion.

"Mary Alice and me."

Her roommate appeared as though the sound of her name had been the cue she was waiting for. Tori stared at her, more confused than ever.

"Don't look so surprised," Mary Alice said, a smile dimpling her cheeks. "Allen and I have hooked up. Where he goes, I go."

Allen looked both pleased and embarrassed at the same time.

Tori glanced from one beaming face to the other. Life gets more like theatre every day, she reflected. Allen and Mary Alice of all people! Impossible. But at least one of her questions had been answered. Now she knew what Allen Saunders had been doing in their hallway on Friday night.

Mary Alice broke into her thoughts. "Allen and I have been together almost every minute this weekend. We've been to see three films. He knows all about how they were made and everything. He even knows the directors' names. I never even thought about directors before. Allen says they're every bit as important as the stars."

"Max will be happy to hear that," Tori commented dryly. She glanced at Allen but he was so wrapped up in gazing hungrily at Mary Alice she doubted whether he'd heard a single word of the conversation.

"Allen got me a job as book-holder for *Banana Boats*," Mary Alice went on, "so I'll be going to rehearsals all the time too. How cool is that!"

"Well below zero, I'd say."

Mary Alice drew her neatly penciled blonde eyebrows together in a delicate frown. "What's with you, Tori? Are you mad at me or something?"

Impulsively, Tori hugged her. "My bad mood has nothing to do with you, Mary Alice. I'm glad you'll be working with us in the play. And I'm happy for you and Allen. We've got plenty of time before we have to leave for the theatre. How be I make us a coffee?"

"That'd be great," Allen said, obviously anxious to be alone with Mary Alice even if only for a few minutes.

In the kitchen, Tori glanced at her watch. There really was plenty of time. He might call yet. Maybe she should call him. But she'd be embarrassed if he'd made other plans. She was so preoccupied with thoughts of Mitch she completely forgot how many measures of coffee she'd placed in the filter. Well, she'd dump in a few cups of water and hope for the best. In a fit of optimism, she added one last cupful of water for Mitch. The very thought of him made her weak in the knees. At the age of twenty-seven, she mused, she seemed to be going through a phase most girls went through in their teens. She must get a grip on herself. But she'd far sooner have Mitch get a grip on her, she decided with a rueful smile.

As she returned to the living room Tori discreetly cleared her throat, and Mary Alice reluctantly disentangled herself from Allen's arms. Most of her fake cupid's bow had been transferred to Allen's mouth. Mary Alice wouldn't have been fool enough to resist Mitch, Tori reflected. But her roommate would never have found herself in that situation. Tori recalled her saying she found Mitch Ames frightening. Maybe she was right. Victoria shivered as she remembered his anger at being rebuffed—though he should have known it was only temporary. His whole face had changed. But even angry, he was still the most handsome, sexiest man she'd ever seen.

While the coffee was brewing, Tori tried to make conversation with Allen and Mary Alice, but with one part of her mind she kept listening for the phone to ring. When it did, she nearly jumped out of her skin. "I'll get it!" she cried, racing to pick it up in the same breath.

"Is Mary Alice home?"

It sounded like the red-headed jockey. Numb with disappointment, she called her roommate.

"Why didn't you say I wasn't here?" whispered Mary Alice. "Keep Allen talking till I get rid of whoever it is."

Tori found it easy to keep Allen talking. All she had to do was mention Mary Alice's name and he was off and running. The only time she'd ever seen him so animated was when he was talking theatre with Max. When, after a few minutes, Mary Alice returned, she gave Allen a kiss on the cheek, and hurried out to the kitchen. She returned, carrying a tray complete with coffee, cheese, crackers and cookies. Tori couldn't recall her ever looking so domesticated. She'd even tied a little white organdy apron around her tiny waist.

"Sure is strong looking coffee," Allen observed. "Oh, well, lots of caffeine to keep us on our toes tonight."

Tori could tell from his expression that he would cheerfully have drunk axel grease if it had come from Mary Alice's pink-tipped fingers.

She half expected his glasses to steam up as he continued to gaze at his new love.

Finally it was time to go. They invited her to go with them and Tori agreed even though she knew they'd rather be alone. She needed their company even if going with them made her feel like a third arm.

They had been rehearsing for ten minutes before Mitch Ames arrived. Max's denouncement at his tardiness was eloquent enough to deserve an Oscar, but Tori scarcely heard a word of it. She was conscious only of the fact that Mitch had arrived with Gloria clinging to his arm. Had her rival won the part she really wanted after all?

5
Hot and Cold Stage Kisses

BY THE TIME THREE WEEKS HAD ROLLED BY Victoria was certain Mitch had no interest in any of the eligible girls in community theatre—including herself. He was growing a thin black mustache for his role and it made him look slightly rakish. He seemed to be concentrating all of his attention on the play.

Mary Alice, surprisingly, still appeared to be totally besotted with Allen Saunders. Poor Allen. There were times when Tori felt she should warn him about her roommate's flightiness, but he seemed to be as happy as Tori was unhappy. She hadn't the heart to spoil it for him. Mary Alice's infatuations seldom lasted more than a couple of weeks, so he was already living on borrowed time.

Even so, Victoria reflected, Mary Alice's liaisons apparently lasted longer than Mitch's. After that first time with Gloria he hadn't been hanging around her. And after being chewed out by Max Greer, he hadn't been late for rehearsal again either.

Despite her disappointment with Mitch as her leading man, the play was moving along surprisingly well. Tori found her lines easy to learn and both Mitch and Allen easy to work with. She was glad to be cutting her theatrical teeth on a comedy. Max kept telling them the more they hammed it up the better. Had she been taking part in a tragedy, Tori feared her tears would have been all too real.

But *Banana Boats* was a lark. Mitch played a naïve young professor engaged in writing a scholarly treatise on the lifestyles of half a dozen prostitutes in the tenderloin district of a large city. Tori played his secretary, and they were staying in adjoining rooms in a sleazy hotel.

Allen had the role of her boyfriend who was highly suspicious of the whole business and kept popping in on them at unexpected times. A young woman named Ellie Blythe was taking the part of the hotel maid. Tori recalled her saying if she got that role she'd really make something out of it. Ellie was certainly being true to her word. Every time she came on, she got laughs from everybody who happened to be around—from prop workers to make-up people. Her appearance alone was startling—a forty-four inch bust above a tiny waist, huge silver earrings swinging from a frizzy black Afro, brown eyes that would melt an ice cube at ten paces. A self-proclaimed sex addict, she was also a thoroughly likeable girl.

Most of the half dozen girls who were playing ladies of the evening looked about as much like prostitutes as a group of small town Sunday school teachers. Allen assured Tori the make-up and costume people could perform wonders. "They'll have to," she'd replied.

The play was blocked now and Tori knew all her stage business as well as her lines. When Max had first mentioned the blocking, Tori had only learned by inference that he meant the various movements onstage by the cast. Once or twice, the director had given her a quizzical look and repeated the instructions. But for the most part he seemed pleased with her performance. Allen had been a tremendous help—whenever he wasn't mooning over Mary Alice. They'd spent many pleasant hours practicing their lines together. A growing sense of camaraderie among all those involved in the production made them seem like members of one big family.

The whole gang enjoyed a great laugh over Mary Alice's first attempts at being book-holder. Instead of giving the actor the correct cue, she'd shouted from the wings, "No, no, no. That's all wrong!"

It was the second scene in the third act that troubled Tori most. In this scene, Mitch, the professor, had to pull off her fake glasses and kiss her passionately on the mouth. They'd run through it several times, but Max was dissatisfied. It was almost as though he could sense she was holding back. Tori knew, though, if she didn't hold back the entire cast and crew would know how she felt about Mitch. She trembled when he touched her, his breath on her cheek as sweet as honey. Holding herself aloof from his stage kiss was the hardest part of the play where she was concerned.

Max finally decided her lack of response was Mitch's fault. Flinging down his book, he leaped agilely up to join them onstage. "Good God, man," he roared, "don't hold her as though she's a side of frozen beef! She's a woman, a warm, eager, loving woman. Treat her like one. Like this."

Tori felt herself being swept up in Max's surprisingly strong arms. He tilted her body back and pressed his mouth against hers, locking her into a position of total surrender. His lips were cool and firm, not at all unpleasant. Even as he kissed her, she marveled at the strange chemistry of sexual attraction between men and women. If Mitch had been holding her this way, she would have melted in his arms. With Max, it was easy to concentrate solely on technique. They finished the scene together, and everyone applauded when it was over.

"We'll break for coffee now," the director announced, looking inordinately pleased with himself. "I want you all back here in fifteen minutes. Exactly fifteen minutes. When you do this scene next time, Ames, do it right."

Victoria made herself an instant coffee and carried her mug to a deserted corner at one end of the green room. She wanted to get away from the others, get away from everything. But minutes later Mitch was easing his long frame into the sofa beside her. "Why did you turn off the lamp?" he asked. "It's dark in this corner."

"I want to be in the dark," she replied.

"Don't worry, baby. You are."

"Is that supposed to be funny?"

"Simmer down. I was just trying to be amusing. You looked as though you could use a laugh. I wish you'd quit being so uptight. We're never going to get that scene right till you relax. I know I came on too strong with you, Tori, and I'm sorry for that. I wish I could turn back the clock and start again. I really mean that."

Tori stared down at her coffee. She wished she could press a button and make her attraction to Mitch disappear as quickly as it had come. But even as she wished it gone, she knew she wanted him to stay, wanted to give him another chance even though she sensed she shouldn't. It was an impossible situation. "Maybe I should drop out of the play," she murmured half to herself.

"Jesus, Tori, you can't quit!" He reached for her free hand and she was overcome by his earnest tone as he continued. "You're perfect in the part. Perfect. We'll get that kissing scene straightened out. God knows I'm willing. I haven't managed to forget you, Tori. I've tried, but it's just no use. I keep thinking about you, about the night we kissed for real. I thought we had something good going on."

He lapsed into silence and she turned to him, her eyes brimming with tears. "Me, too, Mitch," she whispered. "That's why I didn't want to go too far too fast."

"Let's get together after rehearsal," he urged. "Meet me at the Sinners Cellar. Maybe Miss Grouchpot will still be there. We'll start all over, act as though we've just met. Please say yes, Tori."

"I'm not interrupting anything, am I?"

The voice was high and strident. Victoria looked up to see Penny Murray—a girl who was playing one of the prostitutes. Even in the dim light, Tori could see she was extremely agitated.

"I wouldn't want to interrupt a cozy little love scene or anything," the girl went on, her voice rising to a dangerous pitch. "If you'd rather be alone, all you have to do is say so."

"We'd rather be alone," said Mitch.

"You bastard!" she shrieked. "You goddam rotten good-for-nothing son of a bitch!"

A number of onlookers had begun to gather around them, silently watching the proceedings. Mitch appeared to be unruffled. "Hell hath no fury," he drawled. "Now would you kindly get lost."

Penny Murray took a step closer to him. She certainly didn't look like a small town Sunday School teacher now, Tori reflected. Anything but. She looked ready to spit in Mitch's face. Tori held her breath.

When the girl spoke again her voice was low and controlled. "My mother always told me if you lie down with dogs you get up with fleas." With that, she turned on her heel and left them.

In the awkward silence that followed, Mitch tried to laugh the whole thing off. Victoria could tell, though, he was deeply embarrassed. A few chuckles escaped from their small audience and she felt unaccountably sorry for him—even though she knew he probably deserved some part of the girl's tirade. "Let's get back to rehearsal," she said. "Our fifteen minutes are up."

6
Scene in the Sinners Cellar

TORI ARGUED WITH HERSELF AS SHE DROVE slowly towards the Sinners Cellar. Go home, the voice of reason kept telling her. Don't be a fool. If you find yourself alone with him again, there'll be no turning back. Profit by others' mistakes. He must have treated Penny Murray shabbily to cause such an outburst on her part. How could anybody be crazy enough to still want a guy like that?

But maybe it wasn't his fault, the voice of her emotions argued. Maybe Penny had assumed something she had no right to assume. In any case, she could have discussed the matter privately. She didn't have to make a big public scene like that. Everyone had been tense for the remainder of the rehearsal, and it had gone badly. After calling down the wrath of every conceivable god upon their heads, Max had called it quits twenty minutes earlier than usual.

"How many ulcers have you got now, Max?" one of the stagehands demanded.

"None yet," he'd replied. "That's why we're quitting now."

"Ask him how many he's caused," someone called out.

A little ripple of laughter followed the remark, but it wasn't enough to restore any real feeling of solidarity. Tori was surprised to find so many people thinking ulcers were caused entirely by stress rather than a virus, but she felt no need to add to the comments. In any case, stress certainly didn't help. She hurried out of the building without once looking back, feeling she wanted to be alone.

But now she was weakening. As she approached the small parking lot of the Cellar, she slowed down. Perhaps she could stop in just long enough to have one drink with him. He'd looked so terribly downhearted. Maybe he had a right to tell his side of the story. But what if she went in and he wasn't there? He might be too embarrassed to face her. Then she saw his red Jaguar gleaming under a streetlight and her indecision vanished. She parked in the nearest vacant space and went downstairs into the club, her heart pounding like mad every step of the way.

He rose to welcome her from the table they'd occupied the first time they'd come here. Her breath caught in her throat as he stood up and reached out to take her hands in his.

"I'm so glad you came," he murmured, looking into her eyes as he squeezed her fingers. "I was afraid you might not after that girl's pack of lies about me."

"Well, I'm here. Now tell me what that was all about."

"There isn't much to tell. I took her out to dinner one night and we fooled around a bit afterwards. I was trying to get you out of my system. But it was no use. It didn't even come close. She left in a fury when it wasn't working for me."

When the young waitress greeted them with her "Wadda ya want?" they both laughed. The girl stared at them as though they'd suddenly gone mad and backed off a little.

"I think I'll have a beer," said Mitch. "A Blue. How about you, Tori? Light rum and 7 Up?"

She was pleased he'd remembered, but she shook her head. "I'll have a Dubonnet. With a twist of lemon."

"How do you mix that?" the waitress asked.

Tori grinned. "You don't mix it. You just pour it."

When they were alone again, Mitch glanced around the dark red room. "Isn't it perfect!" he said. "Everything's the same as it was on our first date. Just exactly the same."

Victoria studied the half dozen men slouched at the small doorway. "Except for one thing," she said. "The blonde man isn't here."

"What blonde man?"

"He was sitting at the bar and he looked really familiar to me, but I couldn't remember where I'd seen him before."

"If you keep talking about another guy, you're going to make me jealous."

"That's rich, coming from you. I saw you with Gloria hanging onto your arm that night."

Tall Stuff

The bitter words has slipped out almost of their own accord, and Tori was glad the young waitress was slapping down their drinks just in time to change the direction of their conversation.

"Tori," Mitch began, "I have a special favor to ask of you. It's rather personal."

"Ask away."

"Would you mind switching those high heels you wear for something lower? You're almost taller than me when we're on stage."

"I'll think about it," she replied. "Okay. I've thought about it. The answer is no. I love my high heels."

"More than me?"

"Absolutely. No contest."

After another drink and a lot of safe talk about the play they were ready to leave. Tori was pleased to see Mitch give their waitress a generous tip to make up for the last time.

Mitch walked Tori to her car, one arm clasped loosely around her shoulders. The night was unseasonably warm with a moon so large and orange the parking lot looked like a stage setting. Tori felt more than a little light headed and she knew it had nothing to do with anything she'd had to drink. The clear voice of reason hadn't entirely disappeared, but she decided to ignore it. Allen and Mary Alice had the right idea. Grab your happiness while you could. Besides, maybe things would be different between her and Mitch. Maybe she'd be able to hold him where others had failed.

Mitch followed her in his sports car. At the first red light, he pulled up beside her, rolled down his window, and honked three times. Victoria was certain he was shouting the words "I love you" in unison with the blaring horn. She drove the rest of the way home with an almost unbearable sense of anticipation. Would he ask her into his apartment? She'd die if he didn't. She couldn't wait to be alone with him. This time she wouldn't spoil everything by holding back.

They parked and walked together through the foyer towards the elevators. Still no invitation. When they reached the door of her apartment, a desperate Tori took the initiative. "I'd like to ask you in, Mitch, but Mary Alice and Allen might be..."

"No problem," he said. "We'll go to my apartment."

Half an hour later, Victoria was removing her clothes in his bedroom while he sat watching her from the edge of his king-sized bed. She was surprised at her own lack of modesty; it was as though she'd lost all sense of restraint. She felt gloriously voluptuous, gloriously wanton. Somehow the fact he was still dressed added to her excitement.

When the last of her clothing lay in a heap at his feet, he groaned and pulled her roughly against his eager mouth, easing her finally onto the blue bedspread beside him. She kept kissing him, burning from his nearness, wanting him more than she had ever wanted any man.

"I'll get undressed," he murmured.

"No!" she cried. "Do it like this. I want to do it like this."

"But…"

"Please. It's exciting this way. It's something I've never done before." She reached for his zipper. "Please, Mitch?"

"Okay, baby. Whatever turns you on." His sweater brushing her bare breasts, he moved quickly on top of her. She was more than ready for him.

Tori's excitement soon carried her to a fever pitch, and she cried out as she reached an early climax, something she'd never experienced before. It was several seconds before he lay exhausted beside her.

"You're one strange chick," he said at last. "I've never made love with my clothes on before."

"I guess it made me feel like, I don't know, like a slave girl or something. A fantasy." She could feel her face burning with the confession. "It was good, wasn't it, Mitch?"

"Mm, better than good. But just wait. You ain't seen nothing yet, as the old show biz expression goes."

Tori chuckled. "How long will I have to wait?"

He rolled over to roughly nuzzle her neck. "Just long enough for me to get out of these clothes."

When at last he stood naked before her, he reached down to turn on a table lamp. "Now we'll do it my way," he said.

Tori marveled at the swirling pattern his brown chest hair made against his slimly tapered body. "You're beautiful!" she exclaimed. "Truly beautiful."

"Isn't that word usually reserved for the female of our species?"

Tall Stuff

"Maybe. But it shouldn't be. Because you are."

When he reached for another Trojan and stretched out beside her on the bed, she smiled and said, "You're still wearing your socks."

"So what?"

"So take them off."

"Why?"

"Because I want you to. I don't want you to be wearing anything at all except that Trojan."

"But you're still wearing your earrings."

"I'll take them off. And you take off your watch. And that gold chain. And your ring."

When there was nothing further they could remove from their bodies, Mitch made love to her again. He was true to his word. It *was* better than she could have imagined.

When she went into his bathroom, Tori opened his medicine cabinet out of sheer curiosity. Two bottles of oxycodone. Why would he need so many painkillers? He seemed to be in good physical shape. Maybe they were just leftover prescriptions. But why two bottles? She couldn't ask him. He'd know she'd been snooping around. But the sight of them troubled her.

It was four o'clock in the morning when Tori unlocked her door and let herself into her own apartment. She moved quietly, afraid of waking Mary Alice. As soon as she switched on the light, she saw a pink envelope propped beside their telephone on the hall table. It was addressed to her in Mary Alice's peculiarly ornate handwriting.

7
Surprise in a Pink Note

TORI HAD TO READ THE NOTE THROUGH TWICE before its message sank in. Even then she could scarcely believe the words she was reading. Mary Alice eloping with Allen! It was too incredible for words. Still she should have known the affair had become pretty serious when Mary Alice had come home with that tattoo of the theatrical masks of Comedy and Tragedy outlined in black on her right shoulder. "The little red heart beneath them symbolizes my love for Allen," she'd told Tori, blushing as she spoke.

They were flying to Ireland for their honeymoon. Seems Allen had a great-uncle there who was always asking him to visit, a great-uncle Allen had never seen. They were sorry about the play but certain Max could easily replace them. According to Allen, Derek Osborne, who worked on lighting, knew the part of the boyfriend as well as he did.

Tori groaned as she closed her eyes, picturing Derek. The fact that he was super effeminate didn't bother her. But his breath! Worse than the bottom of a parrot cage. How would she be able to do that final scene with him?

You were wrong, Allen, she said to herself as she folded the pink note over and over. The play's title of *Banana Boats at Midnight* does have something to do with the play. Everybody in the production is going bananas. You run off with a randy young sexpot, I hop into bed with a man I scarcely know, and poor Max really will go bananas. Losing a bookholder is one thing, but losing one of the leads three weeks before opening night is a disaster.

Tori tucked the note back into its pink envelope, slid it into her purse to show Max, and went into her bathroom to floss and brush her teeth. She was tempted to go back and tell Mitch about Allen and Mary Alice, but another good-night would have been anti-climactic in the literal sense of the word. She'd never dreamed a man could be so insatiable. Or so beautiful. She smiled, remembering, and her mind was filled with only thoughts of Mitch's lovemaking and its effect on her as she switched off her bedside lamp and crawled under the covers.

But soon her mind was traveling in other directions. Mary Alice's parents would probably not be too unhappy she'd chosen to elope. With five daughters to raise, the expense of one less wedding would doubtless give rise to cheers rather than tears. But May Alice and Allen? Well, they always said opposites attract. It might turn out to be a truly happy marriage. With all her heart, Tori wished them well.

She would at some point, she reflected, have to look around for another girl to share the apartment with her. It was too great an expense for her to carry alone for more than a few months. But she wanted to put it off as long as she could. It would be relaxing to have the place all to herself for awhile, good to be able to see an uncluttered kitchen, to use the bathroom without running into a forest of wet lingerie, to hang up her coat in their front hall closet without picking up half a dozen hangers from the floor. She hoped Allen knew how to cook. A person could live on love for just so long. Still, Mary Alice might surprise both of them. Motivation made all the difference. Small wonder it was considered of prime importance in murder trials.

How her mind was wandering! Tori pounded her pillow into a comfortable shape, closed her eyes and made a determined effort to fall asleep. It was useless. She found herself thinking about her family, feeling the sadness that always came when she considered how far apart they'd all drifted since her mother's demise. It had reached the point of Christmas communication, the odd birthday card, and very little else. Her older sister had been first to go; she'd married an American and was living in San Francisco. Tori had visited them after their second son was born, returning to Sunfield distressed by a feeling of envy she couldn't quite shake off. Rita had everything a woman could ask for—a loving husband and a house filled with the laughter of children. She sometimes wondered if Rita realized just how lucky she was.

Her brother Bill was doing his own thing in Calgary, whatever that thing was. She hadn't heard from him in almost a year. Their father and Nora had re-located to Halifax. The men were seldom first to get in touch; it was always up to Rita, Tori, or Nora to maintain contact.

She shivered, recalling her mother's long and ultimately futile battle with breast cancer. She'd been extremely close to her only son. Maybe that was the reason Billy avoided contact with the family. Maybe he didn't want to be reminded. Not that the three of them had anything against the second Mrs. Walker. She'd been as good a stepmother as she knew how, even trying to play matchmaker for Tori. Definitely not one of her skills. But Tori's father seemed happy. That was all that really mattered. Happiness. Intriguing abstract noun. She found herself mentally crooning the words to an old tune. "It seems that happiness is just a thing called Joe." Only the name "Joe" was replaced by the name "Mitch".

Funny she should remember that old song. The jazz-loving boyfriend had been long forgotten, but the old tunes remained in her head. We're all collectors in one way or another, she mused. He had collected vintage records; she had collected their sounds, sounds that were forever stored in her memory bank.

Victoria didn't want to add to her collection of past lovers. Promiscuity was alien to her nature. She wanted permanence. Even though she was crazy about Mitch, she wouldn't have given herself so freely if he hadn't said he loved her—though he'd only shouted it from his car as they were driving home from the Sinners Cellar. The blaring of his horn had almost drowned out the desired words. Tori tossed and turned and finally drifted off to sleep, trying to convince herself she'd be able to hold Mitch by virtue of the fact she wanted him so much. Victoria Ames. The two names went together perfectly.

8
Victoria Speaks Up for Mitch

"You'd bloody well better be kidding!"
Max's voice over the wire was highly explosive. Tori was glad she'd decided to break the news to him by telephone rather than telling him about Allen and Mary Alice in person. She'd even been tempted to send him an e-mail, but that seemed to her too cowardly.

"I'm not kidding, Max," she said when he reached the end of a long rant. "He and Mary Alice have eloped. Isn't that a lovely old-fashioned thing to do! Aren't you happy for them?"

"I'd like to throw rice," he growled, "done up in ten-pound bags."

"Max, you don't mean that."

"Yes, by God, I do. Allen's always been so *professional*. How in hell could he walk out on our play at this late date?"

"Love, Max, love. That thing that makes the world go around."

"I thought that was money."

"Come on, Max."

"Well it sure made Allen go around. Half way around the world. Ireland, did you say?"

"That surprised me too. Saunders is not an Irish name."

Max sounded a little calmer. "I think he once mentioned something about a great uncle he'd never seen living there. Allen's a quiet guy—but a person you could always count on. I still can't get over his taking off like this. We'll have to start looking around for another actor to play the part of your boyfriend."

Tori wrestled with her conscience. She wasn't looking forward to following Allen's suggestion. "Max," she began hesitantly, "the note says Derek Osborne knows the part by heart."

"Derek? The fellow on lighting?"

"That's the one."

"Okay. I'll give him a call. Tori...?"

"Yes?"

"Thanks for letting me know right away. I'm sorry I blew up like that. I know it wasn't your fault."

She laughed. "Maybe it was, in a way. I introduced them."

"Promise you'll never introduce me to anybody."

"I promise."

Tori smiled as she replaced the receiver. In spite of his temper tantrums, Max could be a darling. All the same, she dreaded Wednesday night's rehearsal. She had become far more interested in doing a good job in the play than she had ever thought possible. It was easier to understand now why getting certain roles meant so much to so many people. *Banana Boats* had been going so well. It would break everyone's heart to see it go down the drain now.

As it turned out, Allen hadn't overestimated Derek's ability to do the part. As she'd feared, his breath was the worst problem she had to face. Face it she did though, armed with an inexhaustible supply of candy mints to offer him before their kissing scenes. Sometimes he took one, sometimes he didn't.

If anybody was giving her real trouble, it was Mitch. He kept quietly urging her to ignore Max's instructions and play the role the way *he* wanted her to do it. She didn't want to hurt Mitch's feelings, and she was aware he had a great deal more experience in theatre than she. But she didn't feel right going against Max's wishes. After all, he was the director. Mitch had never made so many suggestions when Allen was with them.

After rehearsal on Thursday night, Gloria invited all the cast and crew to her house for a party.

"You really believe in giving lots of notice, don't you," said Ellie Blythe, silver earring dangling as she shook her Afro. "I'm in a black mood, but I'll go anyway."

"Very funny," observed Gloria as Ellie giggled at her own witticism, being the only black person in the company. Gloria winked at Max. "It's a surprise party," she went on. "My husband's going to be surprised when we get there."

Victoria stared while the others laughed. She hadn't thought of Gloria as a married woman. Neither apparently, had Gloria. Maybe they had one of those open marriages. Tori couldn't understand anybody wanting a set-up like that. That sort of arrangement was *too* open to suit her. One person or the other always seemed to fall out of one end of it.

She squeezed Mitch's arm affectionately, but if he noticed, he gave no sign. Tori swallowed her disappointment. Sometimes he acted as though there was nothing going on between them. She was hurt and bewildered by his behavior but couldn't bring herself to talk to him about it. Maybe they could find a quiet corner at the party and she'd broach the subject. Some guys hated any public display of affection. He might be one of them.

"You look as though you're a thousand miles away."

Max Greer's voice broke into her thoughts and she turned to him, grateful for the small attention. He was talking about the play, as usual.

"Derek seems to be getting the hang of the boyfriend pretty well, don't you think so?" he went on.

Tori nodded. He'll be just fine. I'm glad he matches my height."

"You're playing the part a bit differently," the director noted, drawing her with him to one side of the stage. "I've noticed a couple of things."

She felt it would be a mistake to tell him the small changes were Mitch's idea, so she remained silent.

"I don't like to interfere too much with your interpretation of the role, Tori," Max continued, "but I must say I liked your earlier performances better. You used to get more laughs than Mitch as the professor; now it's the other way around."

"Perhaps it's just the strangeness of working with someone new," she said, knowing her words lacked conviction.

"Well, let's hope you get back to the old Priss on Monday," Max replied. "She was really into the part."

As he drove her to the party on his Harley, Tori's arms were around Mitch, but her thoughts were on Max Greer's words. Mitch *was* getting more of the laughs now. Could he be working against her? No. She put the suspicion out of her mind. She couldn't love someone she couldn't trust. The play was important to her, but Mitch was far more important. She hugged him tightly, leaning against his leather-covered back, and closed her eyes.

A thickset dark-haired man let them in at Gloria's. When he took their jackets and invited them to make themselves at home Tori decided he must be Gloria's husband. He didn't seem to be her type though. He looked shy and a little puzzled at all the sudden activity.

Unmindful of the skirt draped around her neck and her bright red lace bikini panties, a girl was standing on her head in one corner of the crowded living room. A closer examination provided by one of the stagehands announced her to be Debbie White, one of the women who was playing the part of a prostitute.

"Don't mind her, darling," Derek yodeled above the heavy rock music. "She's just doing it to get attention, don't you know. She does this at every party."

A fat woman turned on him. "You don't have to be so spiteful. She's just practicing her yoga." She gave him a push, causing him to spill his drink. "Watch it, you big cow!" he exclaimed.

"Well nobody could ever accuse you of being a bull!" she retorted.

Derek grinned. "Touche, darling," he said, bending to mop up the drink with a towel Gloria handed him. Then he waltzed off in the general direction of the kitchen.

"Booze is over here," Max shouted. "Every man for himself. Every woman too. An equal opportunity bar."

Mitch had disappeared somewhere, so Tori went over to the kitchen bar and mixed herself a rum and 7 Up. Everybody seemed to be talking at once, and the noise was deafening.

Mitch joined her in time for a second drink, but there was no opportunity to talk. To ear-splitting rock music, six Frosty Prosties, as the cast referred to them, were doing an uninhibited version of an old dance called the bump in the middle of the room. There'll be more than a few bruised buttocks tomorrow, Tori reflected. Mitch appeared to be enjoying the show, and he was doing his best to join in with them. It looked to her like a scene from Dante's Inferno.

A male voice with a decidedly Scottish accent boomed in her ear. "Should flautists all put down their flutes and listen when a *prosti toots*?"

Laughing, she turned to see a familiar looking blond man standing next to her. Where had she seen him before? Of course. The Sinners Cellar. But who was he? Then it came to her in a flash. She knew him from his picture in the *Town Talk* column of the newspaper.

Tall Stuff

"Andrew Macdonald!" she cried.

"Mea culpa. And you're Priss, aren't you?"

"How did you know?"

His clear blue eyes crinkled at the corners as he grinned up at her. "I could impress you by claiming psychic powers, but the truth is I caught some of your rehearsal tonight and Gloria invited me here."

"How did you like the play? Or shouldn't I ask that?"

"No harm in asking. Think I'll save my opinion for my opening night review though."

Tori looked around, but Mitch had disappeared into the crowd. The music was slow and soulful now. Gloria's husband Joe seemed to have gotten into the swing of things. He was dancing with Penny Murray, holding her closer than a miser hold his wallet. Well, at least Penny wasn't carrying any torch for Mitch. Gloria was busily dispensing crackers, old cheese and new kisses in about equal order. Tori noticed she seemed oblivious to her husband's dirty dancing. Seconds later, Max relieved Gloria of her tray and proceeded to show Joe and Penny what it was to dance really close. Tori smiled. It was like some kind of contest between the couples.

"Dance?" Andrew enquired.

She set her glass on a nearby end table and moved easily into his arms. The moved well together. Tori was glad he wasn't trying for the Fast Fusion of the Year Award. Andrew was a few inches shorter than her, but that didn't seem to matter to either of them.

"Let me freshen your drink," he suggested when the music stopped.

Drinks in hand, they headed for a small library off to one side of the living room, furnished with a sofa and a couple of leather armchairs. They sank comfortably into the bright afghan-covered sofa, pleased to have found a quiet corner to talk when the music started again, even louder than before. "I like your column, Andrew, I read it all the time," she began.

"That's good to hear, Victoria. I sometimes wonder if there's anybody out there."

"Andrew, do you remember a play called *Hello Out There*? An older member of our group said they did that one several years ago. I'm not familiar with it, but the title struck me as interesting."

"I remember it all right. I was young and a little arrogant then. I was a bit hard on them in my review. It's a difficult play to tackle."

"I hope you'll go easy on us. This is the first time I've been involved in community theatre. I'm nervous and excited all at the same time."

"That's the way it should be," Andrew assured her. "They say if you aren't nervous you won't be any good. By and large I'd say we have as good a troupe of actors here as you'd find in any like-sized city."

The house was filled with music, conversation, and laughter. Victoria was enjoying herself. Andrew was likeable and interesting; she felt as though she'd known him for years. His wasn't the most handsome face in the world, but it did have a lot of character. She imagined it was the sort of face she'd enjoy painting if she were an artist. He chuckled when she told him that, but for some reason she wasn't embarrassed about sharing the thought. He was easy to talk to. She would have worried about deserting Mitch, but he obviously wasn't concerned about tracking her down.

Inevitably, their conversation returned to *Banana Boats at Midnight*.

"Can't you give me just a wee hint about how you felt about my performance tonight?" she teased.

Andrew seemed to be carefully considering his answer before he spoke. "It's a great comedy," he said finally, "and I think you'll be very good. If Mitch Ames gives you half a chance to be."

Tori was stunned. "What do you mean by that?"

"I mean you're up against a real stage hog. You won't have a prayer if you keep letting him upstage you the way he did at rehearsal tonight."

"I resent that. I happen to think Mitch Ames an excellent actor. Not only that, but he's my boyfriend. He wouldn't do that to me."

"Break a leg then. Or your heart." Andrew's voice was cool now, and Tori struggled to her feet, a knot of anger making her short of breath. She hurried out of the room in search of Mitch.

She found him doing a crazy version of the can-can with a line of the Frosty Prosties. "Please take me home, Mitch," she implored, tugging at his arm. "I have a splitting headache."

9
No Laughing Matter

MITCH DROVE HER, ZOOMING AROUND every corner at a speed that swept away her anger and left terror in its place.

"I suppose that was your way of paying me back for making you leave the party early," she accused, when he finally brought his big red Harley to a screeching halt.

"Don't be childish," he replied, taking the shiny black helmet from her.

"You're the one who's being childish. You haven't said a single word since I told you I wanted to leave. It's not my fault I have a headache."

"Headache, hell. You wanted to leave because the other girls were getting all the attention."

"Mitch, if you think I'm jealous of any of those Frosty Prosties you're out of your mind. If you'd like to know the truth, I wanted to get away from Andrew Macdonald."

"Why? You two seemed to be having a pretty good time."

"He said something I didn't like."

Mitch held the door for her. "You'd better be nice to him," he advised as they walked toward the elevators. "I understand he's the local critic. He'll review *Banana Boats* on opening night. If he does a hatchet job on us, he could kill the crowds for the rest of the week."

"That cuts no ice with me. He said something nasty and I told him what I thought of him."

Mitch pressed the elevator button. "I always make it a point," he said, "never to spit in a well I might want to drink from again."

"Spoken like a true opportunist."

"I'm practical, that's all."

"Practical! Mitch, you're like a plate glass window. You're so easy to see through it's pathetic."

"Well, lady, you can stop looking any time you want."

They entered the elevator, silence like a stone wall between them. They left it the same way. Tori hurried along the corridor and began, with trembling fingers, to place her key in the lock of her apartment door. Too many emotions had been crowding in on her too quickly—anger, then fear, and now this awful chasm between her and Mitch. It was too much. She really was getting a headache. Why did every relationship have to be so damned difficult? What was wrong with her anyway? Why was she being so testy? Did she have a "best before" date stamped on her forehead?

All at once, his hands were on her shoulders. "I'm so sorry, Tori. I didn't mean what I said."

Ignoring him, she pushed open her door.

"Please. Let me come in with you." His husky voice touched her like a physical caress. "Please, Tori. Just for a little while."

"Not tonight, Mitch. I need time to think."

"I need you, Tori. I've been through a bad time. I moved here to make a fresh start in life. My last girlfriend broke up with me. She did it through an e-mail. You can't get much colder than that. For a while there I started swallowing pain pills to numb my feelings. I complained of a bad back to get some pills from my doctor, then took them to make myself feel better. I got over that though. In fact I have bottles in my medicine cabinet I haven't even touched. Not since I got together with you. Please, Tori, don't shut me out."

She looked up into his troubled brown eyes and somehow she was in his arms, his hot kisses making her feel alive again. Her anger dissolved, and she wanted him with a desire that knew no bounds.

"Hey!" he exclaimed. "We'd better get inside before we get arrested. Any more of this and I'll have you down on the floor right here."

Eager now, she led him into her apartment. Laughing like lunatics with every step, and pausing to kiss each newly uncovered portion of skin, they left a trail of clothing all the way into her bedroom.

"Mitch," Tori moaned as he arched her back against him, "don't ever stop. I want you inside me forever."

But she was satisfied long before he shouted her name as his body shuddered in its final thrust.

"You're incredible," she whispered. "I didn't think it was possible for love to be like this. You do love me, don't you, Mitch? You've only said so once, and sometimes you act so indifferent it worries me."

He leaned on one elbow, staring down at her. "What do you mean 'once'? When did I say I loved you?"

"You know. That first night. In the car. We stopped for a red light and you pulled up beside me. You yelled it as you honked your horn three times. I couldn't hear you, but I could read your lips."

Mitch dropped back against the pillows and laughed. Something in his laughter made her feel alone and frightened.

"What is it? What's so funny?"

"You are, baby."

She pulled away from him and he hurriedly went on. "It's okay, Tori. Just an amusing mistake, that's all. I said 'I'll race you' that night. You didn't seem too interested though, so I just followed you home instead. Hey! You're not crying, are you? You know I'm crazy about you."

She forced back the tears that threatened to betray the depth of her anguish. She even made an attempt to join him in the small sounds of laughter he seemed unable to control.

"Of course I'm not crying," she managed at last. "It is rather funny when you think about it. Guess I'm just a hopeless romantic. Very out of fashion in today's world."

He pulled her close to him. "Very much *in* fashion with me. I really get it on with you, Tori. You know that. You're like a big tall real-life baby doll. Just don't forget to take your pill tomorrow. We can't be too careful."

Suddenly Tori wanted to be alone, wanted it so much she couldn't hide her impatience. "You'd better go now, Mitch. It's very late."

"Why can't I sleep here?" he mumbled, snuggling closer to her.

She felt no responsive warmth for him. His laughter had wounded her, and the wound still smarted.

"I want you to leave," she insisted.

"But it's nice and comfy here, and I'm sleepy."

"Mitch, from now on, I don't intend to spend the night with anyone except the man I marry."

He jumped out of bed. "You just said the magic words, baby. I'll be running along. Nothing personal. I just don't want to get tied down by holy matrimony yet. Not for a long time yet."

Tori heard him scrambling around for his clothes, but she stayed put, blankets pulled up to her chin. When she heard the door close, she got up and locked it. Then she put out the lights and went back to bed. For a long time she lay awake, wondering how she could possibly love a man she didn't even care for all that much. Cupid had made her fall in love with the wrong person. She'd like to grab his arrows and stab every one of them into his plump little backside.

10
Guess Who's Calling?

THE SHRILL RINGING OF HER TELEPHONE awakened Tori early the next morning. Still half asleep, she padded out barefoot to answer it. The man's voice on the other end sounded familiar, but she was too drowsy to place it.

"Who is this?" she repeated. "I'm really not interested in playing guessing games. It isn't even daylight yet."

"Some big sister you are! It's months since we've talked and this is the kind of welcome I get."

"Billy!"

"The same. How are you, Tori?"

"Fine. I'm fine, Billy. This is a surprise. Where are you calling from?"

"Would you believe the bus depot?"

"You mean here—right here in town?"

He chuckled. "If your voice gets any higher, Tori, you'll be in that range only dogs can hear."

"I can't help it. I'm so surprised. I can't believe you're really here in Sunfield."

"I've come to visit for a couple of days, Sis. I've got something to tell you."

"Tell me now."

"No. It'll keep till I see you."

"Get yourself a coffee at the bar and I'll be there as soon as I can. What time is it anyway?"

"Six-thirty."

"Okay. I'll see you in twenty minutes or so."

Tori's mind raced as she ran around her living room pulling on the blue tee shirt and jeans she'd worn the night before. What could Billy be doing in Sunfield? She hoped he wasn't in any kind of trouble. He hadn't sounded unhappy though. Just the opposite. She brushed her hair quickly, touched her lips with pink gloss, added a pair of bright green hoops to her ears and went to the fridge for a small tub of yoghurt.

The morning traffic seemed to be moving at a snail's pace as she drove towards the bus depot. Each red light was like a conspiracy directed against her alone. She could scarcely wait to see her brother again. Too bad Rita lived so far away, she reflected. It would be wonderful if the three of them could get together. She wondered whether Bill had changed much since she'd last seen him. She must remember not to call him Billy. He'd always insisted on Bill. Smiling, she recalled the words of the song their grandma used to sing to him. "Oh, where have you been, Billy Boy, Billy Boy?" She hummed the tune as her tires sped along the asphalt. "Oh, where have you been, charming Billy?"

A wife, she thought suddenly. Maybe that was it. Maybe Billy had taken a wife. Well, she'd know soon enough, she thought, as she pulled into the parking lot at the depot. She opened the car door, tried to jump out, and grinned as the seat belt held her fast. More hurry, less speed, she told herself.

Before she'd taken a dozen steps, he was dashing toward her, his sun-bleached hair feathering in the breeze, his smile familiar—a little older now—whisking her back through time.

"Billy Boy!" she cried.

"Long tall Sally!" came his shout in return.

Their old teen-age nicknames gave rise to unabashed laughter as he dropped his duffel bag to give her a quick hug. She kissed his cheek and drew back to look at him. "It's so good to see you."

"You, too. It's been too long."

"Now tell me. What's the big surprise?"

"Come on. I'll tell you on the way. Where's your car?"

She led him to her shiny green Ford and they piled into it, both talking at once.

"Rita and Jason send their love," he said as they pulled out into the street. "I've been down to see them. Her husband's a really nice guy. Took me all over San Francisco. And their kids are terrific. Getting big now."

Tall Stuff

"Growing like weeds, as Mom used to say. Now tell me your news."

"I'm going to Haiti in ten days. I wanted to see you before I go. And I'd like to spend some time alone with Dad, too—if I can pry him loose from that woman he married."

"Billy, like it or not, that woman is your stepmother. Don't be so hard on her," she admonished. Then his words sank in. "Haiti! Why in the world are you going there?"

"To work. On construction. Those people need all the help they can get after that terrible earthquake a few years ago. I'm going with a group and we've signed up for two years."

"That's altruistic of you."

"You're not the only do-gooder in the family, Tori. I'll fess up though. I have my eye on one of the girls in the group."

Tori remained silent for a few seconds, digesting the news. "But Haiti's so far away," she said at last.

"Well, you know me, Sis. I always wanted to see the world. Tori, I haven't been much to keep in touch, but that doesn't mean I don't think of you often."

She glanced at him, and a rush of memories overwhelmed her. "I'm glad you're here. We've got a lot of catching up to do."

Over coffee, they reminisced about their childhood days, doing jigsaw puzzles together, making homemade fudge, riding their bikes to the lake, skateboarding in the park, going out to trick-or-treat on Halloween. He was always a super hero—usually Batman, Spiderman, or Superman. She never tired of being dressed as a Red Cross Nurse.

"Everything changed when Mom got sick," he said.

"Our childhood came to an end," she agreed.

They were interrupted by the doorbell. Tori left him to answer its summons. A delivery boy greeted her with a smile and a large bouquet of yellow roses. The card tucked into them read simply: "For the Leading Lady in my Life, Mitch". Not even Love, Mitch. It would take a lot more than a few roses to make up for the way he'd laughed at her.

Tori gave the boy a conspiratorial wink, dug into her purse to hand him a five dollar bill, and ripped the card in half. "Take them to Apartment 2018," she said. "That's where they're meant to go. To a man who's madly in love– with himself. Tell him so."

That gesture should speak louder than words she decided as she closed the door.

"What was that all about," Bill asked. "I couldn't help overhearing you."

"Nothing," she replied. "Nothing important."

For the next couple of days, up until the moment Bill left, Tori scarcely gave Mitch Ames a second thought. She was too busy taking her brother around town, introducing him to her best friend right Kate and her darling godchild. And telling him all about the play she was taking part in. Their time together fairly flew by, both of them promising to stay closer in touch using Facebook to make it easy.

Early Monday evening she answered her door to see Mitch standing there, his dark eyes surveying her with an expression that was part hostility and part something she couldn't quite define. "Want a lift to rehearsal?" he enquired.

"I'd almost forgotten about it," she answered, "along with forgetting you."

"Small wonder. I see you've been, shall we say, preoccupied." His words were laden with sarcasm and she realized with some amusement he'd seen her with Billy and was jealous. Some perversity made her withhold an explanation.

"Well, do you want a ride or not?"

"I'll drive myself, thank you. Now if you'll excuse me…"

"Come with me, Tori. It looks like rain and there's no sense in taking two cars."

"All right," she agreed, "but only in the interest of cutting down on air pollution."

"Good. I'll be back in fifteen minutes. Be ready."

"Yes, sir!" she replied, executing a snappy salute.

He smiled then, and Tori found herself thinking of the first time she'd seen that smile. Not so long ago, really, but it seemed like a long time. She hated to admit it to herself, but the physical attraction was still there. If anything, it was stronger than ever. Damn him anyway.

11

Max Greer's Heart to Heart With Tori

THE FIRST HALF OF THE REHEARSAL WAS A NIGHTMARE. Tori had forgotten to bring mints, and Derek's breath left her gasping for air. Mitch kept forcing her to play with her back to whatever audience they might have until Max threatened him loud enough for everyone to hear. The Frosty Prosties seemed to be experiencing a collective loss of memory; it reached the point where the prompter was reading more lines than the actors were saying. When Tori somehow skipped an entire scene in the third act of the play, she felt she had either to laugh or cry. She chose to laugh.

"You won't be laughing two weeks from now," roared Max, "when you get up on that stage and make a damn fool of yourself."

The laughter turned to tears, and Tori felt herself teetering on the edge of hysteria. With that, Max ordered everybody up to the greenroom while he had a private talk with her.

He began by offering her a cigarette. When she shook her head he put one arm around her shoulders and led her over to the stage sofa to sit next to him. She was surprised someone so close to her in age could be so like a father. He talked gently to her till she was calm again, explaining he understood how hard it was for her to learn to work with someone other than Allen. "But don't let Mitch bully you," he cautioned. "I know how you feel about him, I guess we all do, but you'll have to learn to stand your ground with him or he'll run away with every scene you do together. You can do a great job when you put your mind to it, Tori. Remember that. I picked you because I had faith in you. I still have. Okay, Priss? Feel better now?"

Tori nodded. She did feel better. Max had a peculiar quality of being able to make her feel either on top of a mountain or deep in the lowest pit. That was probably what made him such a good director, she decided. He knew how to manipulate people. But maybe manipulate was too strong a word. He understood people.

The rest of the rehearsal went smoothly, with the cast giving their all. The book-holder had very little prompting to do as they went through each scene with renewed enthusiasm. Even Derek's breath seemed to improve a little. Tori began to feel a keen sense of personal satisfaction as they moved steadily towards the final climax. Mitch was playing the part as he had in the beginning, and the difference it made was truly remarkable. Their kissing scene presented no problems now. In fact Max had to tell them to break when she and Mitch spent a little too much time on it. But he chuckled when he hollered, "Time to call it a night, kiddies!" and Tori knew he was well pleased with their work. The old camaraderie was back in full force by the time they finally broke up.

"Let's stop at the Cellar for a drink before we go home," Mitch suggested as they waved good-night to everyone and got into his car. "I think we deserve one after that performance, don't you?"

"What is it you like about the Cellar?" Tori asked.

"I don't know. Maybe all that campy red plush. Or that grouchy waitress. Or the fact they don't have any entertainment during the week. You've got to admit, that's a real plus."

She laughed. "Most of the time, yes."

"I want to stop there tonight for a special reason," he went on. "Something very important to both of us."

Tori pressed him for further details all the way to the club, but he would tell her nothing.

When finally they were settled with drinks in hand, she asked again. "What special reason, Mitch?"

Before he could reply, Andrew Macdonald came out of the men's room and walked leisurely towards them. Tori hoped he wouldn't stop, not because she was still angry with him, but because she was consumed with curiosity about what was on Mitch's mind.

"Hey, Andrew!" Mitch called out. "Over here."

Tori forced herself to smile as Mitch invited the columnist to sit down and have a drink with them. Now she would have to wait until she and Mitch were alone before they could talk. She couldn't help wondering why he had asked Andrew to join them. Would he have been equally friendly to someone not involved in the media? She didn't think so. The word "opportunist" came unbidden into her mind, and she toyed with her swizzle stick without looking at either of them.

But, as before, Andrew Macdonald proved to be an excellent conversationalist. Tori forgot her previous irritation with him as they exchanged ideas. He had a biting wit, but it was backed up by a warmth that took the edge off his most caustic remarks on the available offerings in the entertainment field. The talk turned from plays and films to books, and though she felt disloyal, Tori couldn't help noticing how much more knowledgeable Andrew was than Mitch. She supposed she was being unfair. After all, Mitch was an engineer and no doubt competent in his field. It was strange, really, that he never said much to her about his work. Perhaps he wasn't very interested in it himself.

"Well," said Andrew, rising easily as he grinned down at them, "I'll be on my way. It was good talking to *you* again, Tori."

Flushing slightly, she mumbled something and glanced at Mitch, but he appeared not to have noticed any slight on Andrew's part. She was suddenly filled with love for Mitch. He seemed so open, so vulnerable. Glad they were alone again, she reached across the table and took his hand, twining her fingers into his as she studied his perfectly proportioned face. "I shouldn't say this," she murmured, "but you're so good-looking it fills me with wonder. I don't think I've ever in my life seen a man as handsome as you."

Looking pleased with the compliment he began, "Now it's time to tell you my reason for wanting to come here tonight. I feel like this place is sort of special to us. That's why I wanted to give this to you here."

He took a ring from his pocket. The modest diamond winked at her in the dim light of the Sinners Cellar. "When I saw you with that guy this week-end," he said, "I realized I was in danger of losing a good thing. No. Don't stop me, Tori. If I don't do this now, I might get cold feet. I'm asking you to marry me."

"Oh, Mitch."

"Is that a yes?"

"You...you haven't even said you love me."

"For Christ's sake, Tori, would I ask you to marry me if I didn't?" He set the ring on the table between them. "Of course I do. Here—try it on. See if it fits."

Slowly, she picked it up. It was a bit tight, but she managed to work it over her knuckle and into place. She looked from it to Mitch and smiled tremulously. "Let's name the date," she said, "I can hardly wait to tell my family."

"Hey—there's no big rush, is there? Let's just keep this our secret for now. At least until the play's over."

Tori's mind was racing. She'd need plenty of notice for her dad and Rita. She wanted her wedding to be a family affair. Of course, Billy wouldn't be able to come. The thought of her brother gave her pause. Should she tell Mitch he was the "guy" he'd seen her with? No. Why spoil everything? She'd tell him years from now, and they'd both have a great laugh over it. "Let's get out of here, Mitch," she said. "Let's go home and have a real celebration."

Several hours later Tori lay staring into the darkness as she twisted the ring round and round on her finger. Mitch had been at first surprised, then furious, when she'd asked him to leave after they'd made love. "But we're engaged now," he'd argued.

"Yes," she'd replied. "But we're not married."

The ring was beginning to feel uncomfortably tight. She tried pulling it off, but couldn't get it past her knuckle. Why hadn't he checked with her to see what size she wore? Could it have belonged to another girl? After all, new rings came in boxes. Maybe someone had thrown it back in his face. She recalled the scene in the greenroom with Penny Murray. He'd probably left a trail of broken hearts behind him. Maybe he'd moved to Sunfield to get away from his past.

Tori tossed this way and that, trying vainly to keep such imaginings out of her mind. Maybe she should have let Mitch spend the night, she mused. Then she'd be safe in his arms, safe from the thoughts that were forcing themselves on her now. She wished she could trust him. Without trust, she told herself, you have nothing.

Finally, she got up and ran cold water over her finger until she was able to remove the thin golden band with its sparkling diamond solitaire. Only then was she able to fall asleep.

12
Good Advice from a Good Friend

EARLY THE NEXT AFTERNOON, feeling the need for some serious girl talk, Tori left her engagement ring in the bathroom and drove over to visit Kate. The two women talked while the baby slept.

"I'm just not sure about what I want," Tori was saying, aware that she sounded more like a teenager than a woman of twenty-seven. "Kate, I've never told a living soul this, but Mitch is the first man I've ever reached orgasm with. I was able to get there on my own, but never with a man. I was beginning to think I was frigid. Does that surprise you?"

Her friend silently studied her, and Tori felt herself flushing under the steady gaze. Finally, she spoke. "That's not as unusual as you might think, Tori. I was the same way when I first got married. I tried to make the right passionate sounds so Bob wouldn't know, but for the first year or so it just wasn't happening for me."

"No kidding!"

"I didn't really enjoy sex until after I had Dana. But I always knew I loved Bob. You sound uncertain about that. Are you maybe mistaking lust for love?"

"Sometimes I think I am. When he looks at me with those chocolate brown eyes I melt. I want to rip his clothes off then and there."

Kate smiled. "I guess you're not frigid."

They laughed easily together. Kate rose to pour each of them a cup of strawberry herbal tea. "From what you've told me," said Kate, "he seems to be pretty wrapped up in himself. I've only met him the once that time when the three of us met for coffee, so I shouldn't judge, but I got that impression. I agree with you about one thing—he does have looks to die for."

"He's like a vulnerable little boy at times. Maybe that's part of his charm."

"That kind of charm can wear pretty thin when it comes to marriage."

Tori decided to say nothing about the engagement ring. She needed more time, she told herself. Time to be certain she and Mitch could find happiness together—somewhere other than in bed.

"Kate, how did you know Bob was the right man for you?" she asked.

"That's hard to answer. I just *knew*. We both did. I don't even recall the exact words of his proposal. But the first time he said he loved me I knew I felt the same way about him. I also knew I'd be a golf widow a lot of the time. Maybe I'll take up the game myself after we spend a few years raising a family. I threw away my pills because we want another baby as soon as possible."

"Maybe you'll have a boy next."

"Well, you know what they say, as long as it's healthy. But to get back to your dilemma, Tori, are you asking me if I think Mitch Ames is right for you?"

"I suppose I am, yes."

"Is he considerate? Does he make you feel good about yourself? How is he in the compliment department?"

"I got a left-handed one the other night. We were lying in bed and he said I'd have a perfect figure if only my boobs were bigger. Or words to that effect."

Tori sighed, remembering. He'd tried to make up for those words by smothering her in kisses, but somehow the remark still rankled. She couldn't bring herself to tell Kate that Mitch seemed to be stealing her scenes in the play. Or that he'd never told her he loved her, not in those three all important words. Kate would think her a fool for going on seeing him, and she'd be right.

"To wax poetical," said Kate, "if you're in doubt, throw him out."

Despite her frustration, Tori chuckled. "That's not exactly what I wanted to hear, but I appreciate your honesty. Give this to Dana when she wakes up," she added, pulling a large pink and yellow rattle from her handbag. "It sounds like bamboo wind chimes," she said. "Listen."

The two women hugged each other and Tori took her leave, more confused than ever about her future.

13
Beside a Field of Buttercups

THE VERY NEXT TIME THEY MADE LOVE, Mitch said the words Tori needed to hear, said them over and over. "I love you, too, Mitch," she murmured.

After a week's time, the diamond ring fit her perfectly. She began to wonder if she was losing weight from so many sleepless nights. Even though he wanted to keep their engagement secret for a time, Mitch was certainly proving he cared in the way he knew best. And there was no doubt in her mind about her feelings for him in that department. The play was going well. She had no misgivings about her imminent return to work at the hospital. The break was all she'd needed to restore her enthusiasm for nursing.

She felt closer to her family than she had in a long time. Without telling Mitch, she shared the news of her engagement with them. They'd sounded truly happy for her. Rita had promised she and her family would come to Sunfield so she could serve as her matron-of-honor. Nora and her dad declared they wouldn't miss it for the world. Billy sent his best wishes via Facebook. Everything seemed to be going her way. Why then did she continue to have bouts of insomnia, to feel vaguely dissatisfied. It didn't make sense.

On Saturday, she decided to go shopping. Maybe looking at wedding gowns would cheer her up. She knew exactly what she wanted—something along classical lines in gleaming white satin. Preferably strapless.

She was probably being silly, Victoria told herself, wanting to wear a white gown and carry all the trappings that had once signified virginal purity. But a dream was a dream, and she'd always pictured herself in bride's finery, a bouquet of mixed flowers trembling as she glided majestically down the aisle on her father's arm. A long lean Queen Victoria she thought with a smile.

She'd ask Reverend Dawson, the Unitarian minister, to perform the ceremony. She'd joined the church because her friend Millie at the hospital was a member, but she'd been to services only a dozen times in the past year. However, Jerome Dawson was a dedicated and understanding man. She was certain he'd give the words the ring of sincerity they needed.

It wouldn't have to be a large affair—just their closest friends and immediate families. Good God! Immediate families. She'd given no thought at all to Mitch's family. He was an only child and his parents lived in Edmonton, that much she knew. But how would she get along with them? From the little he'd said, she'd gathered they were a trifle snobbish. But what did that matter? She was marrying him, not his parents.

Getting married. The words had a strange sound to them now. "I'm getting married," she said aloud. But even the vocalized words sounded unreal to her. It had all happened so fast. Perhaps that was why it was so hard to believe. Trying on wedding gowns would give it the concrete touch it needed. She'd go to Marchand's first. They always had a good selection of women's apparel. They were one of the few shops in town that catered to tall girls' needs and Tori bought most everything there. Vain or not, she couldn't help thinking that she and Mitch would make a fabulous looking couple. She might even wear flats. Silver ones.

As Tori dressed, she found herself wondering if she should ask Kate to go with her. It would probably be difficult for her friend to get a sitter on such short notice. Anyway, she wasn't quite ready to tell Kate about her engagement.

Despite her zany ways, Tori found she missed Mary Alice. The apartment was always neat now, but except when Mitch was with her, it was always empty.

A frosty autumn morning greeted her as she left the building and walked briskly towards her car. Under an overcast sky, the maples bordering the parking lot were exchanging their green leaves for pale yellow ones. Fall, and everything dying. Tori sighed, trying to change the direction of her thoughts. When you stop growing, you start dying. What a depressing idea. One doesn't have to stop growing though, she told herself. At least not mentally. It might get a little more difficult, but it wasn't impossible. She'd seen elderly people leave the hospital so full of the joy of living they made her feel growing old wasn't so bad after all.

By the time she'd tried on three gowns Tori knew she'd made a mistake in even thinking about her nuptials. She simply couldn't get into the mood, and trying to force it was making her even more depressed. She'd heard there was a new exhibition of watercolors at the art gallery. She decided to go and see it.

An hour later, Tori was lost in the contemplation of a painting of a mother and child in a field of buttercups when a voice at her elbow startled her.

"I like that one too. A summer's daydream caught under glass."

She turned around to find her own face inches away from Andrew Macdonald's.

"Drew!" she exclaimed.

"That pleases me," he said, putting away his notebook and pen. "Only my friends and family call me Drew."

It surprised Tori that the name had come so suddenly to her lips. She must have been using it on a subconscious level for some time. In the next moment, she wondered why she should have been thinking of the journalist on any level.

"It's for sale," he went on, if you've got four hundred bucks lying around."

"I think it's worth it."

He laughed. "So do I." He glanced at his watch. "I've been covering this show for the paper and I'm about finished. It's a quarter to twelve. How about joining me for lunch?"

"I'm not really hungry."

"Then at least have a drink with me on this cold grey day."

"It is miserable, isn't it," she agreed. "Maybe a drink is just what I need."

As they walked across the street to the Baxter Arms, Tori wondered why she had so readily agreed to accompany him. She felt a little guilty, but the desire to spend some time with the journalist outweighed any sense of wrongdoing.

Tall Stuff

When they'd fully discussed the art show, their talk turned to little theatre. "How's the play coming?" he asked.

"Shaping up pretty well. It had better. We've only a week left. I get butterflies just thinking about it."

"This is your first time on stage, isn't it?"

She drained her glass, then looked across into his questioning blue eyes. She liked the rows of little lines that fanned out from the corners of them. Laugh lines. Why lie to him? "How did you know?" she asked.

"You're not like the others. You're different from the usual community theatre regulars."

"You talk as though you don't like them very much."

He finished his drink and leaned back. "I guess they're okay. But they seem pretty phony most of the time. And they have such fragile egos."

"It's different when you're in a play with them," Tori argued. "You really get to know them then. They're actually a lot of fun. The other night I admired a sweater Derek was wearing and he said, 'Do you like it? I knitted it myself.' He even offered to make one like it for me. How can you help responding to people like that?"

He grinned. "They're so damned promiscuous though. Derek's had half a dozen lovers in the last couple of years. And the others are just as bad. Jesus, Tori, I know I shouldn't gossip, but Gloria must have slept with every leading man she's had in every play for the last five years. I don't know how her husband puts up with it."

"Live and let live, that's my motto."

"And a good one it is. But why do they insist on calling every roll in the hay a meaningful relationship. I mean who are they kidding? Themselves?"

"Sounds as though they've made you a sort of Father Confessor."

"Only because I do a lot of PR work for them. And try to give a fair review of every play. Even the one-act ones they do at their building."

He paused to order another round of drinks. When the waiter left, Andrew ran a hand through his sandy blonde hair and grinned ruefully across at her. "Don't mind me. I'm just a sour old bachelor. Maybe I'm jealous because I can't be that casual myself. A couple of years ago, I called it quits with a live-in girlfriend. I wanted marriage and children. She didn't. I suppose I thought she'd change her mind. She wouldn't.

Said she saw enough of kids teaching school all day. I appreciated her honesty, but we didn't want the same things in life."

There was a sadness in his eyes now, and for the first time Tori found herself at a loss for words. Finally she mumbled something about his not being as old as all that. She studied his face. It was still boyish in some ways, yet lined and weather-beaten and wise beyond time. She wondered just how old he was.

"I'm twenty-nine," he said, as though reading her mind.

The waiter came and deposited their drinks in the silence that followed. Tori took a few sips of her rum and 7 Up and found herself feeling a trifle lightheaded. "I like being with you," she said suddenly. "You're good company."

"You are too, Tori. There's something in you that brings out the conversationalist in me. I'm not usually this talkative. I'm probably boring the hell out of you."

"Quite the contrary, Drew. I'm glad we ran into each other today."

"Beside a field of buttercups. Tori, do have lunch with me. They have a good dining room here. Great salad bar, too. Smoked oysters and shrimp included."

"Well…" she hesitated, hands under the table as she twisted her ring round and round. But what could be the harm in having lunch with a friend? She was hungry now, and she didn't want to eat alone.

"Do your good deed for the day and say yes," he urged.

"Yes," she said, and finished off her drink.

They had eaten like a pair of stevedores and were relaxing over coffee when the trouble began. It started innocently enough—with the discovery they were both fans of the poet Robert Burns. Tori quoted for him her favorite lines: 'Then catch the moments as they fly, and use them as ye ought, man; believe me, happiness is shy, and comes not aye when sought, man."

"Are you happy, Tori?" Drew asked.

"Of course I am," she replied. "Why do you ask?"

"Because most of the time you don't look it."

"Well I am. Mitch and I are engaged. I'm very happy."

Quickly, he reached for her hand. When he saw the diamond, he dropped it. "You didn't tell me about that."

There was a note of accusation in his voice and something else—something she couldn't quite understand. "I've been wearing my ring since we met at the gallery, Drew. I wasn't trying to hide anything."

"Well I didn't notice it. Maybe because the diamond's so small."

"Is that supposed to be funny?"

"It's not supposed to be anything. I just wish you'd told me, that's all."

Tori looked at him and the expression in his eyes told her he'd been interested in being more than a friend. She had behaved badly. She should have told him. She felt a heaviness descend, smothering her light mood. "I'm sorry," she said.

"I am too. I like you, Tori. I was hoping…well, never mind that now. Are you certain Mitch Ames is the right man for you?"

"Of course I am," she lied. "I wouldn't be marrying him if I weren't. You don't think much of him, do you?"

"No. I don't," he replied without hesitation. "He seems to think he's a young Laurence Olivier. But it's none of my business who you choose to marry. Or should I say whom."

"Exactly. It is none of your business."

It was as though a cold wind had blown away every last trace of warmth between them. Tori was as angry with herself as she was with Andrew. He'd put his finger on the one thing that had been bothering her for some time. Mitch's vanity. He'd kept insisting on her wearing flats rather than heels until, tired of arguing, she'd given in to him. And he couldn't seem to pass a mirror without pausing to admire his reflection in it.

"Shall I walk you to your car?" Andrew's voice had taken on a steel edge as he shoved a few bills beneath his coffee cup and picked up the check.

"I'd rather you didn't," she replied, remaining where she was. "I want to stay here for a little while."

"Then I'd better get back to the paper." He started towards the door but returned briefly to her side, his voice softer when he spoke again. "I wish you good luck, Tori. I really do. I have a hunch you're going to need it."

14
A Phone Call Cut Short

AFTER ANDREW LEFT, Tori ordered another cup of coffee. She sat for several minutes staring into its dark brown depths. Then, moving like an automaton, she stirred sugar and milk into it and lifted the cup absently to her lips. What an insufferable man, Drew could be, with his holier than thou attitude. What right did he have to criticize anyone's lifestyle? So what if Gloria was a nymphomaniac. It was none of his business. She was one of the most refreshingly honest people in the world. She'd confessed to Tori she was deeply involved with Max. Said he was the best lover she'd ever had. Max even read poetry to her. None of her other lovers had ever done that.

Andrew was right in one way though. Victoria knew from talking to the cast members such liaisons rarely lasted longer than the plays they were performing at the time. Gloria was kidding herself if she thought otherwise. Still, what was wrong with living with illusions? Most people did the same thing.

Tori took a sip of coffee and glanced around. The lunchtime crowd had gone, and except for a middle-aged couple in one corner of the dining room, the place was deserted. A wave of melancholia swept over her as her eyes returned to rest on the debris of their meal. She and Drew had been having such a good time until Mitch's name had come up. She'd forgotten her earlier feeling of ennui as she'd listened to him talk, enjoying the pleasant trace of Scottish burr in his voice. Could it be more than that? she wondered. Could she be interested in him on another plane—a physical one? Impossible, she told herself. She was in love with Mitch. Her feeling for Drew was strictly platonic. He was too stubborn and opin-

Tall Stuff

ionated anyway. Even if she did agree with most all of his opinions. And he wasn't good-looking—not in the usual way at least. He wasn't tall enough for her either. In fact in her high heels when they'd danced together at Gloria's party she'd felt as though she towered over him. That feeling hadn't lasted long though. He'd made some joke about always wanting a woman he could look up to and they'd moved easily together, lost in each other and the music.

Impatiently, Tori drained her cup. Why was she even thinking along such lines? It was absolutely ridiculous. She was engaged to Mitch. She dabbed at her mouth with a napkin, picked up her brown leather bag, and went downstairs to the women's washroom.

The pale milky-mauve color assaulted her eyes as soon as she opened the door. It brought with it the memory of coming here as a young nursing student. She and the other girls had often laughed at the garish lavender of the ladies' room, as it was then labeled on a brass plaque on the heavy oak door. Those days seemed such a long time ago. The girl she was then seemed like a total stranger to her now. Some of her female friends had cherished loftier ambitions, but even then Tori had wanted only to meet the right guy and settle down to raising a couple of kids. It had seemed so simple a dream, so easy to fulfill. Work for a few years then settle into marriage. She would have liked her first love to be her last, but like some soap-opera heroine, she'd found out too late he was already married. His part of the dream had already come to pass. A house in the suburbs and a couple of kids. She must have been hopelessly naïve. But at least she hadn't been gullible enough to believe him when he'd said he'd eventually divorce his wife if only she'd give him enough time. Even if he had meant it, she wouldn't have wanted to be the one to destroy another woman's dream. After months of self-inflicted exile, she'd fallen into the waiting arms of the collector of vintage records. Hard to tell even now what went wrong there. They'd been so much in love with the old songs, with the whole world, with each other. But gradually they'd found themselves becoming completely out of tune with one another. Breaking up had been a mutual decision. It was the music she remembered best.

Tori stared at her face in the gilt-edged mirror. The light glancing off the mauve walls gave her features an eerie cast. She recalled the first corpse she'd ever seen, a little white-haired woman who'd died in her sleep, mouth wide open like a baby bird waiting to be fed. She shivered and turned away from the mirror without bothering to repair her make-up. She didn't care if she had raccoon eyes from the tears that had spilled over despite her attempts to blink them away.

As she made her way up the stairs, Victoria was overcome with a desire to talk to Mitch. She'd never phoned him at work, but surely he wouldn't mind—just this once. She really felt the need to connect with him. She dug into her bag for her cell phone and called as she made her way up the stairs. The coolly efficient voice of a secretary informed her that Mr. Ames was on another line. Would she like to hold? Yes, she would.

It seemed to her an endless wait, but it was only a couple of minutes before he picked up the phone. "What is it?" he asked abruptly. "Tori, I'm in a helluva rush."

"I just wanted to hear your voice."

"What?"

"Nothing, Mitch. Nothing at all. I'll see you tonight."

She stuck the phone back in her bag and walked across the empty lobby to retrieve her coat.

The grey day seemed even greyer than ever when she emerged from the Baxter Arms and began walking towards the art gallery where she'd left her car. She felt so drained of energy it was an effort to go on putting one foot ahead of the other. Mitch's brusqueness had hurt her, but it was Andrew's level blue gaze that haunted her as she got into her car to drive back to her empty apartment.

15
What is This Thing Called Love?

TORI SAT BESIDE A LARGE WINDOW in the hospital cafeteria, an untouched dish of rice pudding in front of her. It had looked good when she'd picked it up, but after struggling through a grilled cheese sandwich, she felt unable to swallow another bite. With her spoon, she toyed with the dessert's nutmeg topping.

"You'd better eat it," a female voice behind her commanded. "You're getting to be nothing but skin and bones."

Victoria turned to see Millie Johnson studying her, a frown creasing her already well-creased forehead. She couldn't think of anyone she'd rather see. Millie's solid presence was always a comfort—from the top of her bunned-up blue hair to her white orthopedic oxfords.

"Sit down with me, Millie," she invited. "You're the very person I wanted to see."

"Sure I won't be intruding? You seem to be miles away. What are you doing here anyway? You're not due back for a couple of weeks, are you?"

"That's right, but I can't stay away from the place I guess. You know how it is. The hospital's our second home. Millie, I'd really like some advice if you have a few minutes to spare."

"Age does not necessarily bring with it great wisdom, my child."

"I'm serious, Millie."

"Then I'm at your service. I've already had my lunch and I don't go on duty for twenty minutes. We still miss you up in Maternity, kiddo." She sat down and busied herself in fishing a peppermint out of her pocket. "My never-ending supply of sweet drugs," she quipped.

"Millie, how can you tell if you're really in love?"

The question seemed to pop out of its own accord, and Tori realized it had been nagging her for some time. Her body tingled whenever she thought of sex with Mitch, but her mind seemed to be warning her not to mistake lust for love.

"Couldn't we start with something a little easier? Like solving climate warming, for example."

"I'm afraid not."

Millie shifted the mint from one side of her mouth to the other. "I guess being in love is wanting to be with someone as often as possible," she finally replied. "Like if you see a good movie or a beautiful sunset or something and the guy you love isn't there to share it with you it, well, it detracts from the enjoyment of the occasion. That sounds crazy, doesn't it?"

"No, it doesn't. I remember when I was a kid if I had a chance to go someplace special and my best friend wasn't with me it wasn't half as much fun."

"Well, that's it. The man you love should be your best friend. Take Jack and me. We've been married almost thirty years now, but we still share things like a couple of kids. And you know the most important thing of all? Laughter. We've had so many good laughs together. Got us through the tough times of raising three boys, I can tell you. The mischief they'd get into!" She fell silent, a far-away look in her hazel eyes.

Tori stopped toying with her spoon. Come to think of it, she and Andrew had laughed together more often than she and Mitch had. She'd even shared more laughs with Max if it came to that. She and Mitch seemed always to be either making love or bickering. She'd behaved coldly towards him after he'd been so abrupt on the phone but he'd known how to melt her iciness. He always did. A few passionate kisses was usually all it took.

"Another thing," Millie went on, warming to the subject, " I watched that old movie on telly the other night—*Love Story*. In it the guy or the girl, I don't remember which, said 'love means never having to say you're sorry'. Well, in my experience, it's just the opposite. Love means never *hesitating* to say you're sorry."

"I think that makes more sense," Tori agreed. She was thinking of Mitch's lack of apologizing for his brusqueness when she'd called him at work. He'd sounded almost rude.

Tall Stuff

"Why all this soul-searching anyway?" the older woman asked.

For answer, Victoria held up her left hand and waved it back and forth.

"You're engaged!"

Quickly, Tori lowered her hand. "No so loud. I'm not ready to announce it to the world at large." She glanced around the busy cafeteria, relieved that no one seemed to be paying them any particular attention.

"Why keep it a secret? You should be shouting it from the rooftops, as they say. Besides, I'd like to give you a shower or a Stag and Doe or whatever they're doing to celebrate an engagement these days."

"I don't know, Millie. I don't know my own mind. I'd rather you didn't say anything just yet. Okay?"

"Sure, kid. I'm no blabbermouth. I understand. If you really need some good advice, maybe you should go and see Jerome Dawson. I know you like him. He's not one of those uptight ministers who thinks he has all the answers. I went to talk to him when we were having problems with our oldest boy and he was such a help, so understanding about teenagers. Of course he and his wife raised three of their own, so they've been through the troubled teens and he knew where I was coming from. I think he's the reason my husband and I became Unitarians. And since you've been going whenever you can, I know he'd be willing to try to help."

"Thanks for the suggestion, Millie, but I don't think I could do that. I'd be embarrassed to talk to anyone about this except to you and my friend Kate. Women are easier to relate to somehow when it comes to the subject of love. I can't talk to my family. They all think it's high time I got married, so I've told them nothing other than the fact that I'm engaged. You've been like a mother to me, Millie, ever since I started working here."

"You've been like a daughter to me, Tori. The daughter I never had. We've been through a lot together. I was so cranky when I quit smoking you bought me a bag of mints and told me to chew and cheer up. Remember?"

"I do. Guess I made you switch addictions."

"This one's less harmful."

"That's true. I feel hungry now, Millie. I'll eat my dessert and fatten up."

"Good. Dig in."

Tori took a spoonful of the rice pudding and confessed, "Sometimes I think I fell for Mitch mainly because he was taller than me and had looks to die for. I still get teased about my height. Believe it or not, some people still come out with that tired old question, 'How's the weather up there?'"

"Next time that happens tell them it's raining and spit on their head to prove it."

Tori laughed. "If only I had the nerve to do that. It would serve them right."

"Often the simplest things in life seem like the most difficult. I wish I could be more help, Tori, but remember you have your whole life in front of you. You don't want to make the wrong decision."

"I know that, Millie. I'm so mixed up lately. Maybe it's just too much excitement. Remember when I called to tell you I was taking part in a play? Well, dress rehearsal is coming up soon—Monday night, in fact. I've got to get myself sorted out. I've just got to."

"I'm looking forward to seeing your debut. I'll bring a good-sized cheering section with me. Every friend and relative I can round up. Tori, take my advice for what it's worth. Leave all this heavy thinking until the play's over. Your head will be a lot clearer then. Just try to relax and have fun. Well, back to the babies for me."

Tori straightened her shoulders. "You're right, Millie. I'm only spinning around in circles this way. It's not fair to Mitch either. I'm glad we talked. I feel much better now."

Victoria smiled as she watched her stocky friend stride away, immaculate in her white nylon uniform. Sad to think she'd be retiring in a few years. Tori would miss her. She had such a marvelous philosophy of life. And her thoughts on marriage made a lot of sense. Victoria wanted that kind of marriage for herself. But would she ever have it with Mitch Ames?

16
A Redheaded Stranger Appears

THE NEXT DAY, FEELING SHE HAD TO KEEP BUSY, Tori gave her apartment a thorough cleaning from stem to stern. She had just carried two plastic bags filled with Mary Alice's discarded Harlequin romance novels out to the Blue Box and was returning to her door when she saw a buxom redhead letting herself into Mitch's apartment. Victoria stopped dead in her tracks and stared at her. She herself had never been given a key to her future husband's door. Why should another woman have one?

The hard-looking woman glanced at her without a flicker of interest in her heavily made-up eyes and proceeded to enter Mitch's apartment. There was nothing Victoria could do but go back into her own place and wait for an explanation. She knew better than to call Mitch at work. He'd made it plain to her wasn't to be disturbed there unless it was a matter of life and death.

All possible cleaning done, Tori turned on the television but found herself unable to concentrate on any of the programs on the many channels, not even the one on the channel featuring the world's tallest people—a girl named Marley who stood ten inches over six feet, a British family with six kids all over six feet in height, and an American boy who grew to be nine feet tall and died at the age of twenty-two. The program was disturbing and she turned it off. What was that redhead to Mitch? Why did she have a key to his place? She was tempted to go there on some pretext or other to find out. Maybe she could go over and ask to borrow a teabag or something. But what would she say if she did confront the woman? She didn't want to do anything that would set Mitch off in a fit of temper. Perhaps she was a relative of his. But why had he never spoken of her? Questions continued to plague. Finally she rose, went to the fridge for a drink of orange juice, and looked at her watch. Four-thirty. Mitch wouldn't be home for another half hour at least. She'd go crazy if she didn't do something. Even going for a walk might help. Anything to get her mind off that woman. If she could feel this jealous, she told herself, maybe she really was in love.

Victoria decided to walk over to the Sunfield Shopping Centre and pick up a quart of milk. And some cheese. She'd forgotten cheese when she'd done her weekly marketing. The fresh air would do her good—get things back into focus. No doubt there was a perfectly reasonable explanation for the redhead's presence.

It was a beautiful fall day, but the walk didn't help. By the time she reached the shopping centre Tori's head was aching with dull insistence. She ran into Ellie just as she was leaving the food store. The girl smiled broadly, silver earrings dancing beneath her Afro hair-do as she urged Tori to join her for coffee in the restaurant next door.

"I don't have much time," Tori protested.

"Just a few minutes," coaxed Ellie. "Come on. I'd like to talk to you about a couple of scenes in the second act. I told Max I thought it would be more effective if I came running in instead of just walking in when the Professor takes..."

Victoria stopped listening but Ellie continued to chatter all the way into the restaurant, so wrapped up in her role she seemed not to notice Tori's preoccupation at all. She didn't even pause for breath when the waiter brought their coffee, and Tori was able to get by with only occasional murmurs of assent. Her thoughts remained fixed on Mitch. She'd always prided herself on not being the jealous type. Only yesterday she'd agreed with Mitch that jealousy was caused by immaturity. He'd proven his maturity by reacting casually when Tori had told him about her lunch with Drew. Too casually, she'd thought, even though she agreed with him on principle. But principle was one thing; real life, quite another. Here she was, torn apart because some strange woman was in Mitch's apartment. And he wasn't even home. It was ludicrous. Laughing at herself didn't help though. Nothing would help except a logical explanation. Yet how could there be a logical explanation for that woman having a key?

"Well, what do you think?" Ellie asked, pausing for a much needed breath.

Tall Stuff

"Sounds fine to me," Tori mumbled. "Why not try it like that and see how the others feel about it?"

"I *knew* I could make something out of the maid part," Ellie crowed. "I just knew it!"

"You've barely touched your coffee. Look, Ellie, I really don't have much time. I walked over here and I ..."

"Relax. I'll give you a lift home."

"Thanks, but I need the exercise. And the quiet, she decided, sighing as she leaned forward to cup her chin in both hands. There should be something like Alcoholics Anonymous for non-stop talkers, she thought. They could call it *anon anon*.

"You're thinking about Mitch, aren't you," Ellie said, looking pointedly at Tori's ring finger. "Don't look so surprised. Most of us know you two are engaged. Are you worried about the way he carries on?"

"Of course not. Why should I be?" She leaned back and clasped her hands under the table in front of her. She'd forgotten she'd worn the ring. She hadn't mentioned her engagement to any of her fellow actors, but she'd slipped up and worn the ring a couple of times and she knew her silence on the subject was driving them crazy.

Ellie's brown eyes narrowed and her face took on a calculating look. "Mitch sure is amusing sometimes," she said. "He was teasing Debbie White last week—you know, trying to kiss her. When she said his new mustache tickled too much he told her a kiss without a mustache was like an egg without salt. Isn't that a hoot?"

Tori realized her reaction was being studied, so she forced a casual chuckle. "Mitch is always goofing around with the Frosty Prosties, Ellie. "It's probably good for their morale. It doesn't mean anything to him." She pushed her cup away. "I really have to run now."

"Don't be in such a rush. Hey—did I ever tell you about the time Maureen threw a big Halloween party at her house? It was the first time any of us met her husband Phil. Only we didn't *expect* to meet him. And vise versa. Phil always hated the community theatre crowd. Said all the women were phonies and all the men were faggots. So Maureen organizes this party for when he's out of town, eh? He's not expected back for a couple of days. Well, the bell rings just after midnight and Derek goes to answer it. Jeez, you should of seen him—dressed up like a ballerina in flamingo pink tutu with matching pink satin slippers, the whole bit. Anyway, Derek opens the door and Phil's standing there, big as life and twice as ugly. He must have forgotten his key. Funniest thing you ever saw. They just stood there and stared at each other for a minute. Then Phil orders everybody out of his house. I'll never forget the look on Phil's face—or Derek's either, for that matter. He damn near had a heart attack right on the spot."

Tori laughed in spite of her bad mood as she rose and picked up the check. "See you at rehearsal, Ellie." She paid the bill and hurried out of the restaurant.

Damn the luck, she fumed as she made her way home. Mitch would have been back for at least half an hour by now. She'd wanted to meet him in the parking lot so she could talk to him right away.

Before she was half way home, a sharp pain in her side forced Victoria to slow down. She shifted her bag of groceries from one arm to the other and walked carefully until she was able once more to breathe deeply. When finally she reached Mitch's door, the hallway outside it was ominously quiet. She had the feeling even before she knocked that her summons would go unanswered. She pounded on the door just the same, holding her breath as she waited. The silence seemed oppressive. Where could they have gone? Or were they still inside, hiding from her, laughing in one another's arms?

At length she turned away, set the brown paper bag by her own front door, hurried out of the building and checked the parking lot behind it. Mitch's bright red car was nowhere to be seen.

Slowly, Victoria made her way back to her apartment. She poured herself half a glass of milk before putting the carton into the fridge. It would be useless to make a meal, she decided. She had no appetite at all. Switching on the television set again, she settled down in front of it and watched numbly as half-hour segments punctuated by canned laughter unfolded endlessly before her. Every now and then she rose to telephone Mitch, feeling more depressed each time the futile ringing reverberated in her ear. She refused to leave a message. At twelve-thirty, she gave up, crawled miserably into bed and pulled the covers over her head.

17

Definitely Not a Magnificent Obsession

THE FOLLOWING DAY TORI FELT SO ILL FROM LACK OF SLEEP she spent half the morning in bed. Finally, she forced herself to rise. She stared at her reflection in the bathroom mirror. A pale stranger in a pale pink nightgown stared back at her. Soul sickness, she reflected, and went back to her bedroom where the rumpled, still-warm bed beckoned invitingly. Resolutely, she pulled on jeans and topped them with a green cashmere sweater. Then she headed for the kitchen. Start the day with a good breakfast, she told herself. Eat a live toad, then nothing worse can happen to you all day.

Where had she seen that sign? Then she remembered. On somebody's desk at the hospital. Great break from duty she was having! She couldn't recall when she'd ever been more depressed. Where could Mitch have been last night? Why didn't he at least call her? What possible explanation could he have for that? Who was the redheaded woman?

Victoria felt a little better after eating a poached egg on brown toast and downing a couple of mugs of coffee. You've always been a strong person, she told herself. Be one now. She picked up the phone and punched in Mitch's number. The phone rang several times before he answered.

"Hullo," he mumbled sleepily.

"I need to see you," she said. "It's important. Can I come over there now?"

"Sure, Tori. A little later though. I'm not even dressed yet. Give me time to get ready."

To get your story ready, she thought, but her voice, when she spoke again, betrayed no such emotion. "I'll be there in fifteen minutes. Okay?"

"Good enough."

He hung up before she did, and she stared for long seconds at the faintly humming receiver before replacing it. The anger and frustration she'd felt last night had become a cold hard knot in her chest. She could scarcely recall the voluptuous woman's face now, save for the heavily made-up eyes and the sensuous mouth. No doubt Mitch would try to make up some story to pacify her. He was an actor, after all. And a damn good one. He'd told her he'd done several leading male roles in community theatre in Alberta.

The quarter of an hour passed at a snail's pace though she busied herself in doing the few dishes she'd used and tidying the kitchen. When she'd brushed her teeth and hair and applied a coat of glossy rose lipstick, it was time to leave.

Victoria was trembling but determined when she knocked on Mitch's door. She had to know the truth—regardless of where that truth might lead. As she waited for him to answer, she fiddled with her engagement ring.

He looked sleepy and boyishly ingenuous in his blue jeans and black sweatshirt when he finally opened the door. "Come in, love," he said, putting an arm around her shoulders. "Jeez, it's good to see you. You're so beautiful. Listen, about last night—I'm sorry I didn't get a chance to call, but I had to go out and look over a job on that new site our company bought. I met one of the guys there and we went pub-crawling for hours. Just guys, though. No fooling around. Just a boys' night out."

"Cut the crap, Mitch. You're not fooling anybody, least of all me."

His jaw dropped at her harsh tone, and Tori could see it was costing him some effort to find his voice again.

"What's wrong?" he asked.

"Who's your redheaded friend?"

She hadn't intended the question to come out in so blunt a manner, but once the words were spoken she was glad she hadn't bothered beating around the bush.

"What are you talking about?"

"Save your breath, Mitch. Don't insult my intelligence any more than you already have."

Tall Stuff

"Tori, I honestly don't know what you mean. What redhead?"

They were still standing just inside the doorway. Tori felt unable to move, as though her arms and legs had turned to stone.

"Why lie about it?" she asked quietly. I *saw* her. She was opening your door with her own key. *I* don't even have one."

He gave a short laugh. "You must have seen my cleaning lady. I gave her a key so she could come while I'm at work."

"She didn't look like a cleaning lady to me."

"You're starting to sound like a wife already, Tori. A jealous one, at that. I thought we agreed jealousy was puerile."

"When there's no reason for it, yes. But, Mitch, you've never said anything about having a woman in to clean."

With a sweep of his arm, he indicated the well-ordered living room. "Do you think I could keep the place looking like this without help?"

"No, but..."

"But nothing. Look, why are we standing out here? Come in and sit down. I'll get you a coffee. I've just made it and it's still hot. Folgers. The special roast you like. Milk, no sugar, right?"

She wanted so much to believe him she allowed herself to be led into his living room to sit on the hard black leather sofa. "Surely you could have phoned me sometime last night," she persisted, but he had gone into the kitchen where he either couldn't hear her or was pretending not to.

When he returned with the coffee, she noticed his eyes were bloodshot. "You've been smoking pot again, haven't you?" she accused.

He set the mugs carefully on the coffee table before replying. "Did you come over here for the express purpose of starting a fight?"

"Mitch, I wish you wouldn't. Not so often. You know how I feel about that stuff."

"I'm not a slavering dope fiend, Tori. So I use a little pot now and then. So what? Lots of people do."

"Does your redheaded cleaning lady use it too?"

"Oh, for Chrissake!" He sank down beside her, folded his arms across his chest, and stared at the ceiling. "There's no reasoning with you when you're like this."

Victoria picked up the nearest mug and took a sip of coffee. It was too strong for her taste. She made a wry face and set the mug back beside his. She had the distinct feeling Mitch was lying to her about last night, but there was nothing she could do about it short of giving his ring back and calling everything off. She was on the verge of doing just that when he reached over to gently stroke the hair away from her forehead. "Don't look so down, darling. I'm sorry about last night. I just didn't have a chance to call. It was a rush job. Then I didn't want to call from a noisy bar. I wouldn't hurt you for the world," he went on, still stroking her hair. "You know I wouldn't. I love you. That sweater makes your lovely eyes greener than ever. You're so gorgeous. I'm on top of the world when I'm with you. I never thought I'd feel this way again after my last break-up. You've made life worth living for me, Tori. Why would I ever want to fool around on a girl like you? I'd have to be crazy."

Even while her mind was rejecting his words, her body was responding to his feathery light caresses. She tried to hold herself aloof, but he leaned over, cupped her face in his strong hands, and kissed her on the mouth. "Mmm," he breathed, snuggling against her ear, "you smell good. Good enough to eat." He pulled down the zipper of her jeans and began at the same time to run one hand over her breast. She was glad she hadn't worn a bra. "Let's go to bed," he whispered.

"But it's still morning. I'll see you tonight, Mitch. I have some shopping to do."

"I need you, baby. I need you now. Please, Tori. You know I love you. Only you."

Maybe he *was* telling the truth, Tori told herself, feeling weak in the knees as they moved as one into his bedroom. After all, his apartment *was* always spotless. He'd need a cleaning woman to keep it that way. And the woman looked rather hard—not someone he'd be attracted to. She'd been foolish to give her a second thought.

By the time he'd finished undressing her, Tori had put the redheaded woman completely out of her mind. She felt incredibly wanton as Mitch's lips moved over every inch of her body. "You take off your clothes too," she whispered.

"Not yet, baby. You know you like it this way."

There was something rough in his voice, something almost brutal.

"No, Mitch. You get undressed too. That was just a silly fantasy I had, and once was enough."

"Not yet," he repeated, pulling her hungrily against him. "You're still my beautiful slave girl. Just like our first time. Remember?"

She tried to twist away, but he held her fast. For a few seconds, she was almost frightened by his insistence. Then he undressed, and in minutes he was pushing himself inside her as his lips sought hers. She forgot her fear, forgot everything in the driving force she was now rising to meet.

18
Max Hosts an Afternoon Party

BECAUSE SHE WAS DETERMINED TO STICK TO HER RULE of no all-nighters before marriage, Tori woke up in her own bed on Sunday morning. It hit her with the force of a Mack truck that opening night was only two days away. How could she do it? How could she walk out on that stage for five evenings in front of a paying audience? She had no business being there. She was an imposter and it would show in her performance. Andrew Macdonald would say as much in his review. Andrew. Drew. She found herself recalling his eager smile when they'd met in the art gallery. 'Beside a field of buttercups' he'd called it. Then she remembered the hurt look that had clouded his clear blue eyes when she'd told him she was engaged to Mitch, remembered how he'd abruptly left her there.

She wondered if Mitch was up yet. On a sudden impulse, she decided to phone and invite him over for breakfast. She'd make them blueberry pancakes. She hurried to the front hall to call, excited at the prospect of showing off her culinary skills.

He sounded grouchy when he answered on the fifth ring. "Jesus Christ, Tori, this is the only morning I get to sleep in. Anyway, if you weren't so damned stubborn we'd still be in bed together. Look—I need at least another couple of hours of sack time. We're invited to Max's this afternoon, so I'll call for you later. Okay?"

"Fine!" she retorted feeling completely let down. She should have known better than to call him before noon on Sunday. Maybe, she thought, the price she was paying for great sex was way too high. She was torn by indecision. Perhaps it was time to call everything off and give Mitch

Tall Stuff

back his ring. Tell him to put it on his little finger since the only person he really loved was himself. He hadn't even told his parents he was engaged. It didn't sound as though he was very fond of his family. He's described his mother as a shopaholic, and his dad, who was a lawyer, as the world's foremost authority on everything under the sun. But this was the wrong time for a break-up. She should wait till the play was over. Millie's counsel there had been good advice.

Deciding she wasn't really hungry, Tori settled for a glass of orange juice and carried it with her to her favorite chair in front of the television set. No use turning it on, she reflected. There was never anything worth watching on Sunday morning. She sipped the cold juice and stared morosely at the blank picture tube. The glassy reflection of a lonely woman stared back at her. If Mitch really loved her he'd have come over. Still, maybe that wasn't completely fair. He probably needed more sleep than she did. Besides, they'd had a wonderful time last night. Dancing till one in the morning, then behaving like a couple of teenagers as they ordered a huge pizza with all the toppings they could dream up. Mitch amusing her with that old guru joke saying, "Make me one with everything." They'd managed to demolish most of it too. Later he'd been so warm, so affectionate. Mitch could really turn on the charm when he wanted to. Maybe she should learn to accept him the way he was. She probably had lots of faults herself—things that bothered him that he didn't mention.

They were certainly continuing to get along fantastically in the physical part of their relationship. Even the brief fear she'd felt with him earlier last night had somehow increased her excitement in their coupling. Coupling. What an odd word for her to think of. Sounded more like train cars hooking up than people getting together. They'd ended up making love under Mitch's shower, the sound of the water drowning out their high-spirited noises. It worried her in a way that they'd made love in every imaginable way in their two apartments. There'd be precious little left for them in the way of novelty once they were married. They'd already tried every conceivable position. Now there was a contradiction in terms. Conception wasn't an option at the moment. Mitch had told her he wasn't interested in starting a family for at least two or three years.

Tori smiled at her reflection as random thoughts continued to chase each other around in her mind. Of one thing she was certain. Sex would always be good between them. She and Mitch both had healthy appetites for it. She was continually surprised by just how demanding she'd become in that area. If Mitch were here right now, she thought, I'd be dragging him off to bed before he even finished his breakfast coffee.

Tori swallowed the last of her orange juice and took the glass to the kitchen to rinse under the tap. She felt at loose ends, wondering what to do with herself until the time came to go to Max's. Any activity would help to keep her mind off tomorrow's dress rehearsal. Too bad the apartment didn't need cleaning. It was spotless. And she didn't have to hire any titian-haired woman to keep it that way either. No. Better get away from that line of thought. Asking for trouble there. She'd accepted Mitch's story. Let it go at that. What would she wear to Max's? The weather was staying unseasonably warm. Banana belt weather for Banana Boats at Midnight. The play again. It was always at the back of her mind these days, ready to send a chill of nervous excitement racing down her spine. Surely they'd all do a creditable job. The last rehearsal had been very good, very professional. Still, she was glad this play wasn't a Festival entry. That would have made the pressure unbearable.

Finally, Tori sat down at her computer to catch up on some long overdue e-mails to her family.

Practically everyone in the cast was there when Tori and Mitch arrived at Max's large apartment in one of the older buildings in the north end of the city. Derek and his shadow-like lover were busy in the kitchen cooking up batches of German potato pancakes. The assembled company emptied the platters as soon as they appeared, washing down the heavy golden pancakes with liberal amounts of beer.

"Delicious!" Gloria was exclaiming, "but what about my figure?"

"Good thing you don't have to get into a costume tomorrow," Max teased, "but never mind, luv," he added, hugging her, "I adore fat women."

Tori wondered whether Max's good mood would carry over to the next day's dress rehearsal. Not very likely, she told herself. Everyone was just too happy. It was too good to last. Too good by far.

"Somebody put on some discs," Debbie White shouted. "I want to dance."

"Go stand on your head," a male voice replied.

He didn't have to make the suggestion twice. Debbie cleared a

Tall Stuff

corner of the dining room and was serenely balanced upside down in no time at all.

Victoria watched in amazement. "How can she do that after drinking beer and eating all those heavy pancakes? Can you do that, Mitch?"

"Sure," he replied, "but I don't want to show off."

"You haven't as much to show off as Debbie," drawled Max.

"Oh, I don't know about that."

They looked over to see Derek, smiling as he leaned in the kitchen doorway.

Tori was surprised to see that Mitch was blushing. She couldn't ever remember seeing him blush before. His face was almost as red as his sweatshirt.

"Who's for Scrabble?" Max demanded, taking the game from the huge china cabinet lining one wall of his dining room. His question was followed by complete silence. "I'm underwhelmed, kiddies," Max went on. "Well, we'll just have to recruit, won't we. I want three players—you, you, and you, Tall Stuff."

"I should never have told you that story, Max," Tori protested. "You'll have everybody calling me by that old nickname."

"They wouldn't dare. You're their leading lady. The star of our production. Now follow me, you three."

Reluctantly they joined him at the round oak table in the centre of the room. Debbie White regained her feet and drifted off with the others to the sound of music now coming from the living room.

The quartet drew letters to see who would play first. Gloria picked an A, so the initial play fell to her. When she'd drawn her seven letters, she studied them briefly, then put down the word PAYMENT. "Thirty-four!" she shrieked, "plus another fifty points for playing all my letters. Eighty-four! Wow!"

Max went wild while the others laughed. "Nobody can have that kind of luck all the time," he roared. "I've got five times the vocabulary she has, but she beats me every time we play this damn game."

"So why do you always want to play it?" Mitch asked.

"Because sooner or later, I'm going to win. Maybe even this time. Eighty-four or no eighty-four." Brow furrowed in concentration, he hunched over his row of letters and studied them for endless minutes while the rest of them waited in varying degrees of patience. Finally, he ran the word PICNIC down from her word. "Eight-fucking-teen," he grumbled.

"That's not so bad," Tori offered.

"Not bad! Hell, I had to use a blank to get it."

Gloria chuckled as she recorded the score. "Speaking of picnics, Max, do you remember the one you organized last summer in The Pinery? You were like an Italian film director gone mad. You'd persuaded almost every family involved in community theatre to come, most of them did, and it was total chaos. It was a windy day, so windy everybody was rubbing sand out of their eyes. And remember all those big dogs people brought? German Shepherds were leaping about everywhere—grabbing hamburgers right off people's buns. It was absolutely crazy! Babies crying in strollers, sand everywhere, black smoke, garbage flying around. I remember seeing you sitting off on a sand dune all by yourself laughing your ass off."

Max grinned and leaned back, remembering. "It really should have been preserved on film," he said, "entitled A Windy Day by Huron Waters."

"You guys going to play Scrabble or Memory Lane?" Mitch demanded.

With that, they returned their attention to the game. To no one's surprise, Gloria won by a mile. Much later, when they were leaving, Max reached for Tori's hand. "Nervous about tomorrow?" he asked.

"How did you know?"

"I can always tell. But don't worry, luv. If you weren't nervous, you wouldn't be any good."

Victoria thought about the director's words all the way home. If being nervous helped, she decided, she was going to be a smash hit in the play.

19

My Place or Yours?

IT WAS STILL EARLY, only around nine-thirty, when they returned from Max's, so Victoria assumed she and Mitch would spend some time together before saying good-night.

"My place or yours?" she quipped as they got out of his car.

"Tori, I'm really bushed," he replied. "Think I'll call it a night."

She glanced at him, certain he was joking. But one look at his set profile and she realized with a small shock he was quite serious.

"Mitch," she coaxed, "I really need your company for a little while. I'm on edge about tomorrow. I won't be able to sleep unless…"

"It's tomorrow I'm thinking of," he cut in. "We both have to be in good shape for dress rehearsal. Believe me, Tori, these run-throughs can be murder. I'm a vet when it comes to community theatre, so I know what I'm talking about."

"But it's not even ten o'clock. Just for a little while."

"Don't press me, darling. I told you—I'm bushed. After all, I'm not on leave like you. I have to get up early for work, and I have to be reasonably bright when I get there. We've been having too many late nights as it is."

Tori's mounting feeling of hurt was rapidly changing to humiliation and then anger. "Please yourself," she snapped when they reached the elevator. "You always do."

Mitch pressed the black button, and they rode up to their floor, cold silence like a cement wall between them.

Although Mitch made a couple of attempts to talk to her, Tori maintained her part of the silence as they got off at the third floor. She rushed away from him, and in her haste to unlock her door fumbled the key and it fell to the floor. Mitch managed to pick it up before she could get her hands on it.

"I can open my own door, thank you," she said sharply, pushing him aside as she grabbed the key and jammed it into its lock.

He stared at her, brown eyes questioning. "Why all this anger? Don't you think you're over reacting? I don't understand you. I really don't."

Victoria swallowed hard, trying to hold back the tears that were threatening to overflow at any moment. "Mitch," she said slowly, "whenever you've needed me, I've been there for you. Remember how I helped you with your lines? These things are supposed to work both ways."

He curved an arm loosely around her shoulders. "I'll come in," he said, "if you let me bring my alarm clock, my tooth brush, and a fresh shirt for the morning."

"Go to hell," she retorted, slamming the door behind her as an exclamation point.

Her apartment was quiet with the kind of Sunday night stillness that made Victoria feel uneasy. She looked at her watch. Ten o'clock. It would be later than that on the East Coast. Too late to call? She really wanted to talk to her father. Maybe he wouldn't mind if she did wake him—just this once. She hoped Nora wouldn't be the one to answer. She was in no mood for a one-sided half-hour conversation with her stepmother.

She switched on the small lamp by the telephone, looked up the number in her little green book, and called it. After a few seconds, a male voice answered, heavy with sleep.

"Dad, it's me. I know I shouldn't be calling so late. I just needed to talk to you."

"Tori! Is something wrong?"

He sounded wide awake now, and frightened. She was sorry for having disturbed him. Hastily, she assured him everything was fine, she'd simply felt lonely and given in to an impulse to call.

"How's that young fellow of yours?" her father asked. He didn't add that her fiancé should be keeping her from feeling lonely, but the implication was there.

Tall Stuff

"He's fine, Dad. Just fine. How's Rita? Have you heard from her lately?"

"Got an e-mail and pictures last week. Both boys won prizes in the music festival."

"Hey—that's great. And did you have a good visit with Billy? I really enjoyed seeing him again. Did you have fun together?"

"Sure did. He's looking happy, isn't he? Hope things work out for him in Haiti. He's sure smitten with that young woman who's in the group he's going with. Here—your stepmother's awake now. She wants to say hello."

"Victoria," came a thin female voice, "I'm glad you called. We should be making plans about your wedding. We don't even know your young man's name. Now if you could just make up a list of…"

"Nora," Tori interrupted, "I really don't want to talk about any wedding plans. Not tonight. I'm just not in the mood."

"Oh?" The word held a world of hidden questions.

"No. I'm too wrapped up in thinking about the play I'm in. Dress rehearsal's tomorrow, and we open Tuesday night. Wish me luck."

"You know we do, dear. I only wish we could be there to see you. What is it they say in the theatre? Break a leg?"

"Thanks, Nora. Look, I know it's late there. I'd better say good-bye now. Let me just have Dad back for a minute. Okay?"

"Of course."

Her stepmother's voice sounded a trifle cool. Had she hurt her feelings? Tori wondered. Well, it couldn't be helped. She couldn't bear to talk about any wedding plans. Not after the way Mitch had let her down. She chatted a few minutes longer with her father, loath to hang up. Finally, she said good-bye and the connection was broken.

When she'd reluctantly ended the call, Tori felt even more lost than she had earlier. Numbly, she went through the routine of preparing for bed, removing her eye make-up, flossing her teeth. When at last she crawled between the sheets, she gave in to the tears that had been threatening for some time. She buried her face in the pillows and cried as she hadn't cried since she was a teenager.

20

Standard Dress Rehearsal

AT A QUARTER TO FIVE THE NEXT AFTERNOON Mitch stood on the threshold of Tori's apartment, a bouquet of daisies in one hand and a box of chocolates in the other. It was so traditional a peace offering Tori couldn't help smiling and asking him in. When he returned her smile, her eyes were drawn as always to the tiny space between his squarish chalk-white white front teeth, and as usual it held an irresistible fascination for her. Looking like a penitent little boy he flung his gift-laden arms around her and their smiles blended into a passionate kiss.

"I felt rotten all day," Mitch murmured between caresses. "You're still my lady, aren't you?"

"Mitch, you're driving me crazy. Just when we seem closest everything falls apart. Like last night. We'd been having such a great time at Max's party. Then you turned around and spoiled it all by being so cold when we got home."

"Let's not talk about last night. Sometimes I get a little moody. I'm sorry if I hurt you, Tori. Now how about making me one of your special spinach and mushroom omelets? I'm a hungry man." He nibbled at her ear as though giving proof to his words.

"I'd better put these flowers in water first. They're beginning to droop already. She took the bouquet from him and went to get a crystal vase from the top shelf in her cupboard. "They're pretty, Mitch," she called back. They're almost my favorites. Good old dependable daisies. Daisies won't tell."

"Mind if I have a chocolate?"

"Help yourself. Don't spoil your appetite though. We'll be eating soon." She tied a red-checked tea towel around her slim waist and set about making the omelet. "Put some music on, will you, Mitch?" she shouted over the noise she was making in the kitchen. "There are a couple of magazines you can look at while I'm slaving away in here. Some interesting articles in Chatelaine."

"Women's stuff. Want any help?"

"No. I think I can cope."

"Good. I'm useless in a kitchen I'm not used to."

Tori hummed as she worked. She felt as though an intolerable weight had been lifted from her. How comforting it was to feel close to Mitch again, his kisses still tingling on her lips, the pressure of his arms still warm on her shoulders. She found a forgotten bottle of white wine in one of her lower cupboards, so she decided to light a couple of candles and make the modest meal something of a festive occasion.

After dinner, they moved eagerly from candlelight to the soft pink lamplight of her bedroom. When they returned to the table for their after-dinner coffee, Tori found her lace tablecloth splattered with melted yellow wax.

"All in a good cause," joked Mitch, pressing his thumb and forefinger against each flame.

"Don't burn yourself."

"Max will burn both of us if we don't get down to Saxony Hall on time. Finish your coffee and let's go."

"Okay. Just give me time to wash our dishes."

"Leave them."

"I'll just put them in the sink to soak."

"You'll make someone a great little wife," he teased.

"Watch it or I'll make you do them before we go."

"Me? Not a chance. That's women's work."

"Not any more, my love. Not any more."

"Okay." He laughed. "I'll get you a dishwasher. But you can bet your cute little ass it won't be me. Now let's go."

The early evening air was mild as they prepared to leave the apartment building. "What say we take the Harley," Mitch suggested. "Just for kicks."

"Count me out. Those kind of kicks I don't need tonight. I'm nervous enough already."

The scene at Saxony Hall was one of complete pandemonium. The movers were just dropping off the last of the sets on the stage as Tori and Mitch arrived. Everybody was running around like mad, getting things in order.

"I wish we were back in our cozy old theatre building," said Tori. "This place looks so big, so intimidating."

"Wouldn't be much room for a decent sized audience there. That building's for rank beginners putting on plays. Two bit one-act stuff."

Tori didn't say so, but she couldn't help feeling she should have been making her debut in one of those productions.

After what everyone else seemed to consider the standard dress rehearsal complete with misplaced props, temperamental tape recorders, and muffed lines, Max shouted, "Okay, kiddies, curtain time tomorrow's at eight-thirty sharp. The make-up crew will be here at seven. Make sure you are too."

Most of the cast and a number of people who had dropped in to watch the rehearsal left at that point. From a carton near the stage, Tori picked up a pale green program, marveling afresh at the sight of her name listed in the cast of characters. Carefully, she tucked three of them into her straw tote bag. She'd send one to her dad and one to Rita. She glanced about, a trifle embarrassed, to see whether anyone had been watching, but the few people left appeared to be busy with last minute business about the play. She walked out to the lobby and stood staring at the large show board propped there. It was covered with purple cloth, and under the golden lettering of BANANA BOATS AT MIDNIGHT eight-by-ten photos of the stars were tacked. Max occupied a place of honor at the top. His lean angular face looked suitably artistic. She wasn't too happy with her picture. She looked too unnatural, too posed. Mitch's was good though. With his face, she asked herself, what else could it be? The Frosty Prosties resembled a group of high school cheerleaders, and Derek Osborne had posed looking soulful in a black velvet jacket with a flowing white ascot, his curly brown hair tumbling over his forehead.

"Admiring yourself, dear?"

She turned to see Derek in the flesh behind her, surprisingly without his shadow lover.

Tall Stuff

"I think we all need big black mustaches drawn on," she joked.

"Mitch already has one, albeit not a big one."

Tori had the uncomfortable feeling they were both staring at Mitch's picture with undisguised admiration.

"Where's your friend Bryan?" she asked.

Derek looked worried. "He went out to get me a Coke an hour ago and hasn't come back yet."

Before she could reply, Mitch joined them, holding out her jacket for her. "We'd best be on our way, my love. Tomorrow's going to be a big day."

The air was balmy and bright with moonlight. Tori would have liked to stop for a drink, but Mitch seemed so preoccupied she didn't even suggest it. He spoke scarcely a word all the way home.

When they reached her door, she turned to him, frowning. "You're awfully quiet. Anything wrong?"

He gave her an absent peck on the cheek. "I'm just beat. It's been a long day."

"Want to come in for a nightcap? There's some wine left."

"Not tonight, Tori."

"Mitch, I'd like to talk about the play for a few minutes. You've hardly said a word to me all evening. We don't have to indulge in any x-rated exercises or anything."

She expected him to smile, but his face remained set and distant. "Just for five minutes," she went on. "It's only a quarter to twelve."

He took her by the shoulders. "Look here, Tori, Max should get a medal for getting through dress rehearsal so early. Usually, you have to send out for sandwiches at midnight just so you can keep going. Now let's do our part and get a good night's sleep. Any actor worth his salt has to train just the way an athlete does."

"Mitch, it's only community theatre."

He bristled. "I don't look at it that way. You never know who'll be out there watching the production. My attitude is professional. Yours should be too."

She smiled thinly. "Good-night, Professor. See you tomorrow."

Without bothering to go through her usual flossing routine, Tori washed, undressed, and slipped into bed where she lay watching shifting patterns made on her bedroom walls by October moonlight. She'd show him who was professional, she vowed. She'd do an acting job tomorrow night that would knock some of that conceit out of him, knock his socks off. She'd do it her way. Make her friends proud. Impress Andrew Macdonald. She fell asleep mentally going over all her lines in the play.

21
Tell Me Something I Don't Know

VICTORIA FELT ITS UNWELCOME PRESENCE before she even got out of bed next morning. Oh, no, she thought, running her tongue lightly over her lips. Not a cold sore! She hardly ever got cold sores. She couldn't even remember the last time she'd had one. Not today of all days!

She rushed into the bathroom, leaned close to the mirror above the sink and stared at the offending corner of her mouth. "Goddamn it to hell in a wheelbarrow!" she roared. A fine acting job she'd do with a sore mouth to worry about. To say nothing of the way it would look. It wasn't fair. Not fair at all. The heroines in Mary Alice's soupy romances never got cold sores. Or boils. Or sties. Or even toothaches. Why couldn't real life be like that? Well, no point in standing here staring at the thing. She'd better hurry over to the drugstore and get something to fight back with. Bloody thing seemed to be getting worse by the minute.

Halfway to the mall, Tori thought about the kissing scene with Mitch. He'd kill her if she gave him a cold sore. Maybe she could hide it well enough so he wouldn't be able to tell she had one. She'd certainly have to try anyway. Damn the luck. That old graffiti writer was right. Sometimes life is just a bowl of pits.

By six-thirty that evening Victoria was confident she'd won the battle. The medicine had been extraordinarily effective, and a dab of medicated make-up proved a good camouflage. The damned thing was barely noticeable.

Mitch was right on time. She smiled a little as she opened the door. "I'm all set," she said. "Let's go."

He seemed to be examining her face. "You've got a cold sore," he announced.

"Tell me something I don't know," she retorted.

"Look—don't snap at me. I didn't cause it. And watch the kissing scene, will you? We can make it look real without getting too close."

"Don't worry, that'll be easy!" She brushed by him and headed for the elevator, anger giving her jet propulsion. He had to race to catch up.

"You're getting us off to a dandy start," he accused. "Jesus! All I need is a bitchy, self-centered co-star."

"Mitch, if you say another word I'll dump this bag over your head, contents and all. So help me God, I will."

He grabbed her arm as she raised her heavy tote bag high in the air. "Take it easy, Tori. Jesus, you've got a bad temper."

She lowered her arm and stared at him for hard seconds. "I never used to have," she said. "In fact people used to say I was very good-natured."

As they exited the elevator he made an attempt to change the subject, but she brushed aside his idle words and turned to him, questioning.

"Why do you suppose I've changed, Mitch? I mean a person doesn't spend years and years being good-natured and then all at once become a miserable bitch."

"Victoria, this is no time for a serious discussion. We're probably both a little uptight. I'm sorry if I said anything to hurt you."

"You sure didn't say anything to help me."

"Okay. I said I was sorry. Now let's drop it."

They drove in silence to the auditorium and arrived just in time to catch an unscheduled, unrehearsed scene between Derek and Max.

"I can't go on," Derek was wailing. "I simply cannot go on."

The director looked more distraught than Tori had ever seen him. "You've got to do it, Derek. You can't let us all down now."

"What's happened?" Tori asked Ellie Blythe, who was standing nearby already dressed in her maid's costume.

Ellie shrugged. "It seems like last night Bryan went out to get Derek a Coke and he never came back."

The words took Tori to the edge of nervous laughter, but Derek's tear-stained face was too real to allow it. Thoughts flashed through her mind—old jokes about husbands going out for loaves of bread and never returning. She moved to Derek's side and put an arm around his shoulders. "Bryan will be back," she said calmly. "He probably just got nervous about opening night and all. Come upstairs and get into your make-up, Derek. Everything's going to be all right. You'll see."

To everyone's surprise, Derek rose and followed her upstairs. The two of them seemed to be surrounded by a collective sigh of relief.

At twenty minutes past eight, Tori tiptoed to the side of the stage and peeked through a narrow space in the maroon velvet curtains. A large opening-night crowd met her gaze, and she was conscious of the now familiar butterflies-in-the-stomach feeling. The first face to catch her eye was Andrew Macdonald's. He was seated in the centre of the theatre-in the fourth row from the front. For a moment, she had an eerie feeling he was looking back at her. She found herself recalling the warm and wonderful afternoon they'd spent together-and how he'd abruptly left her when she'd confessed she and Mitch were engaged.

"Cut that out!" a voice hissed. "You'll bring us bad luck."

Tori turned to see one of the Frosty Prosties beckoning to her. She took one last glance at Drew and joined the rest of the cast in the wings. As she waited, she wondered whether any of the others were as nervous as she was. Not likely. They'd all been through this before. Most of them quite a few times.

At eight-thirty, the house lights dimmed, the curtains parted, and, after a round of applause for the 'office party' set, the play began.

Victoria crouched in the darkness backstage, watching the others go on and awaiting her own cue with trepidation. What if she should get out there and forget all her lines or faint or something? All those people! And they'd all paid to see this production. She hoped Gloria would be alert in the book holding department.

"Here's Priss now!" boomed Mitch from centre stage.

It was time. She took a deep breath and sailed forth, heart and butterflies' wings beating madly.

Caught in the sudden glare of the footlights, Tori felt like a naked runner in an Olympic marathon. The eyes of the audience became one great, all-seeing eye, and for a few seconds she was terrified her mind would go blank, that she'd fail to recall one single line Priss had to deliver. But when she opened her mouth the necessary words poured forth, almost, it seemed of their own accord. She forgot she was Victoria Walker. She became Priss, body and soul, and she didn't regain her own identity until the first scene was over.

As the ensuing scenes unfolded, Victoria found herself in a new world, but it was a world in which she had to fight every inch of the way. Mitch was making it difficult for her at every turn. He had reverted to his earlier interpretation of the professor, and he was getting more than his share of the laughs. He won't get away with this, she vowed to herself. I'll show him I can act as well as he can.

By the end of the first act, Tori felt physically and emotionally drained. She hurried upstairs to change her costume and watch, with several others, a scene more dramatic than any they'd performed so far onstage. Like two boxers, Penny Murray and a girl from the make-up crew stood facing each other from opposing corners of the brightly-lit room.

"You did this deliberately, you bitch!" screamed Penny. "You made me look a hundred and two. Just because I beat you out for that part you wanted in our last play. You goddamned jealous bitch!"

The other girl smiled. "You're supposed to look hard, aren't you?"

"Hard, yes, old, no." Penny grabbed a mirror from the make-up table and waved it in front of her. "Look at the bags under my eyes! Look at the wrinkles! I'd never have gone on like this if I'd seen myself first. I'll get even with you, bitch. You wait and see if I don't."

Suddenly, Max came striding into the room. "What the hell's going on?" he demanded. "We could hear you two screaming all the way downstairs."

"Ask her," Penny retorted. "Or better still, take a good look at me."

Max looked. "Christ Almighty!" he roared. "You've made her look ancient. Where's Pauline? She's supposed to be in charge of make-up. Terry, go tell her to get her ass in here—fast."

Victoria moved on into the costume room, torn between tears and laughter. Poor Max. First Derek, now this. She wouldn't be a director, she decided, for all the tea in China. That was an old saying of her grandmother's. Funny how expressions heard in childhood come winging back. She sometimes felt like a vessel filled entirely with other people's words and ideas.

Tall Stuff

She hoped Mitch would be easier to play opposite in the second act than he'd been in the first. She realized he was anxious to do a good job, but that was no excuse for him to step all over her lines. She wasn't going to let him get away with it.

When she had dressed and checked her make-up, he appeared at her side. "Love you," he whispered in her ear. Some of her annoyance disappeared.

But the annoyance returned as the play progressed. He upstaged her every time he had a chance. When it was finally over, she found it difficult to keep smiling as they made their first curtain call. Millie and several nurses were there, clapping like mad. Then she caught sight of her friend Kate with her husband in the audience, and it was all Tori could do to keep from waving to them. They had promised to come backstage, though, and when they did, Tori intended to talk them into attending the opening night reception to which the mayor and other local dignitaries had been invited. A good chat with Kate was just the tonic she needed.

The cast took two more curtain calls and withdrew, flushed with excitement, the sound of applause ringing in their ears.

"Did you hear that!" Max exclaimed. "They must have liked it." He looked pleased as several members of the audience came backstage to congratulate him. For several minutes the whole area was filled with sounds of happy pandemonium. But between congratulatory friends, Tori was able to study Mitch objectively. For the first time ever, as he responded to compliments, the smile she'd always found so attractive looked to her to be consummately phony.

22

Town Talk Review of the Sunfield Players

VICTORIA COULD SCARCELY WAIT FOR WEDNESDAY'S EDITION of the paper to come out. As soon as she heard it thump against her door, she rushed to pick it up. As always, Andrew's Town Talk column was easy to find. She paused for a moment, almost afraid to read further than the heading: SUNFIELD COMMUNITY THEATRE GOES BANANAS. She smiled, remembering she had once used those very words herself. Then, holding her breath, she began to read:

The Sunfield players opened their season last night with a rollicking comedy. 'Banana Boats at Midnight' has elements of slapstick humor, it is true, but it succeeds on a satirical level as well. There's something for everyone here. With one notable exception, the part of the Professor, the players lived up to the demands of the production. Teamwork is of utmost importance in a play like Banana Boats. There's no place for a prima donna here—male or female. Victoria Carter's performance in the role of Priss was good; if Mitch Ames had not upstaged her with deliberate regularity, it might well have been great.

Tori slowly let out her breath, read the rest of the review, and folded the newspaper. So it hadn't been her imagination after all. Mitch had tried to steal her thunder. And he'd succeeded all too well, judging by the laughter from the audience. Still, she was surprised Andrew had been quite so hard on him.

She closed her eyes, recalling their first days of rehearsal. Because she was completely inexperienced, she'd listened to many of Mitch's whispered stage instructions—even when they'd been in direct opposition to Max's. She'd been naïve enough to think Mitch was trying to help her.

Tall Stuff

Tori made herself a mug of instant coffee and re-read the review. Mitch was going to be furious when he saw it. The rest of the cast would be happy though. A good write-up in the Town Talk column meant good crowds for the rest of the week. And Andrew had ended on a cheerful note, recommending the play as a good evening's entertainment. Poor Mitch. Nothing would hurt him more than being called a prima donna. Even though he'd brought it on himself, she couldn't help feeling a little sorry for him. Drew's words were awfully harsh—even if they were true.

Mitch was going to need a friend. Maybe a good meal would help. Last night she'd promised she'd make cabbage rolls for him. Her whole apartment was soon filled with the rich aroma of spicy meat and tomato sauce. It was fun having someone to cook for—and being able to make dishes she didn't have time to prepare when she was working.

As she set the table, Tori tried to stop thinking of other hints of narcissism in Mitch—hints she'd pretty well managed to ignore until now. Like the time she'd asked him his sign of the Zodiac. Cancer, he'd said, not bothering to ask hers in return. Or when they'd taken pictures in the park. He'd seen only his own face, not noticing anything of hers until she'd pointed out a couple of details. A healthy ego was one thing—egomania something else. He'd even assumed she'd given up her high heels for him. He'd been disappointed when she'd told him it was because Doctor. Oz had warned that heels higher than one inch could eventually lead to bunions. "Who the hell is Doctor Oz?" had been his furious reply.

Mitch surprised her by arriving right on time, a bottle of red wine in one hand and a happy expression above his neat navy blue suit. He couldn't have read the review yet, she decided, hurriedly tucking the newspaper out of sight on the shelf below one of her end tables.

"Nice of you to try to hide it, Victoria," he drawled, "but totally unnecessary. I've seen it already."

"And you're not mad?"

"I consider the source. What does that old fart know about theatre?"

Victoria felt a flash of resentment. She was uncertain whether it was caused by his use of the word 'old' when he and Drew were roughly the same age or his contemptuous dismissal of Andrew's capabilities as a critic. She said nothing.

"Don't you agree with me?" Mitch demanded.

"Agree about what?" she hedged.

"That Andrew Macdonald's full of shit."

"I'd better check on our dinner," she said.

He followed her into the kitchen. "You haven't answered my question."

The covered pan on the stove was sending out little puffs of steam. Using a flowered potholder, Tori lifted its lid to check on the cabbage rolls.

Mitch slammed the wine bottle down on the table. "Well?"

"He did give the play a good plug," she said at last. "Should make for a full house the rest of the week. I suppose he had to find fault somewhere, Mitch."

He sank down in a kitchen chair, loosened his red striped tie, and removed his suit coat. His chestnut hair was clinging in damp tendrils against his forehead, and his big brown eyes were sad as they studied her. He looked like a little boy—an unhappy little boy. Tori felt like hugging him and telling him everything was going to be all right. But when he spoke again, there was nothing boyish about him, nothing at all.

"Macdonald's gonna get his fuckin' ass in a sling one of these days."

"Mitch!"

"Sorry, Tori. I know you don't like my using that kind of language. You're my sweet, old-fashioned lady. Come here and give me a kiss."

Victoria didn't tell him it was the threat against Drew that bothered her and not the swearing.

"Give me a kiss," he repeated.

"I'll give you a cabbage roll instead."

"I'd rather have another kind of roll."

"Very funny, Mitch," she said lightly.

But he stood and took her in his arms, and the familiar stirring in her groin almost made her oblivious to everything else. "Mitch we don't have time. Max will be furious if we don't get to the theatre by seven. We'll have to eat and run as it is."

Tall Stuff

"Just a quickie?"

"No way. Pour the wine and I'll dish up the food. And before I forget, thank you for the silk flowers arrangement you left by my door the other day. The daisies actually look very realistic."

Tori didn't go on to tell him the truth—that she preferred a half-dead live plant to any artificial bouquet, no matter how beautiful. Perhaps the fake flowers were right for the two of them. More and more she was feeling that their engagement lacked any sense of reality. They hadn't even talked about setting a date yet.

23
Reaching a Final Decision

DEREK'S LATEST LOVE HAD NOT RETURNED by the fourth night of the play, and Tori was rapidly running out of ideas to keep him happy. His breath was worse than ever. She was convinced it was emotionally caused. Not even a truckload of peppermints would have helped. Well, she reasoned, he had put up with her cold sore; she could put up with his breath. Getting him into make-up and costume each night was a problem.

"Come on, Derek," she coaxed. "Bryan's sure to come back tomorrow. He wouldn't miss the big closing night party. You can count on that. Bryan loves parties. He told me so. And by all reports this is going to be one of the best. I hear Bella Farthington's hosting it and her parties are legendary."

Derek's ingenuous green eyes were trusting as he stared at her. "Do you really think so, Victoria? I mean do you really think Bryan will come back?"

She repeated her words of encouragement, hoping that by doing so she might make them come true. Behind them, Mitch grinned wickedly as they all entered the crowded make-up room. "Don't worry, Derek," he drawled. "If Bryan doesn't come back, you can always get something going with Andrew Macdonald. I hear he's dying to get to know you."

Tori swung around, surprised. She felt suddenly that she didn't know Mitch Ames at all, had never really known him. He was like a stranger, an unpleasant, homophobic one. The sooner she banished him from her life, she decided, the better. "If that's your idea of a joke, Mitch, it's pretty sick," she remarked, loud enough for everyone to hear.

Immediately, Derek was on the defensive. "Are you saying you think I'm sick, Victoria?"

Tall Stuff

"Of course not, Derek. You're different, that's all. People who spread lies are sick. People who make remarks like Mitch just did are sick."

In the pause that followed, Mitch calmly combed his hair. "Do you know for certain it's a lie, Tori? Do you know by experience?"

"I won't dignify that with an answer."

"You never see Macdonald with a girl, do you? Except for the time he took you to lunch, that is. Maybe you know something the rest of us don't know. Is that it?"

All eyes were on them now. Victoria felt her cheeks burning, her temper rising dangerously. "Shut your mouth, Mitch. You're just jealous because Drew's got your number. You're getting back at him for dissing you in print about upstaging me. And just for the record, he was right about that."

"Upstaging you! That's rich. Christ, you've been trying to steal this show from me ever since our first rehearsal."

All at once Max came rushing forward to take each of them in hand. "Victoria," he begged. "Mitch. Don't do this. Everything's been going so well. We're all in the same banana boat here. Anything that hurts one of us hurts all of us. You two have been great up until now. You're a beautiful couple. Beautiful to look at, beautiful to know. Now come on. Kiss and make up."

Victoria wanted to hold back and she was certain Mitch felt the same, but Max gave them no choice. He literally shoved them into one another's arms and held them there till they could feel the rapid beating of each other's heart. After further prodding from Max, Mitch gave her a quick peck on the cheek. The rest of the cast shouted encouragement. As Tori moved her face against the slight tickle of his mustache, some of her anger dissipated. But his hurtful words still stung. She realized she'd not soon forget them. If ever. The truth hurts, she thought. Had he spoken the truth? Was she trying to keep the limelight for herself? Even so, his cruelty to Derek, and to Andrew, had been unconscionable. She was certain now of one thing. She and Mitch had come to the end of their relationship. Diasthemas were not always signs of a generous nature—definitely not in the case of Mitch Ames. Thank God the play would be over tomorrow night, along with her so-called engagement. She'd be more than ready for an all-out super celebration.

She would have to pick the right time, though, to give Mitch back his ring. There was no hurry. She'd wait for the closing night party to be over with first. Timing was important in affairs of the heart. Tori was certain now her feelings for Mitch had always been lust—not love. But she hoped they'd be able to part without too much bitterness. He could be hot-tempered at times. Living in the same apartment building might prove to be uncomfortable if he took the break-up badly.

24
A Standing Ovation

WHEN THEY WERE TAKING THEIR THIRD AND FINAL CURTAIN call on closing night, Tori saw a familiar couple waving wildly from side seats a few rows from the front. She squeezed Mitch's hand and, still smiling, spoke to him above the sound of the applause. "Mary Alice and Allen are out there! See them?"

"Where?" he asked, without turning in her direction. "Oh, yeah. I see them now. Some surprise, eh! Guess Allen wanted to find out what he was missing. He'll probably think he could have done the role of the boyfriend better than Derek."

Holding hands, the entire cast bowed one last time and waited for the maroon velvet curtains to cut them off from the audience. As they turned to leave the stage, Tori felt curiously let down. She had expected to feel an overwhelming sense of relief at this moment. Instead, she had to fight a sense of depression so strong it threatened to bring foolish tears to her eyes.

Everyone was chatting excitedly and milling about backstage. She watched the flushed faces of the cast and crew and wondered whether any of them were feeling as she did. It was a feeling she couldn't even begin to put into words. Perhaps it was something like the post-partum blues. She'd seen enough mothers go through that in her days on the maternity floor at the hospital.

"Come on," said Mitch, suddenly coming up behind her. "We can see Allen and Mary Alice at the party later. They'll be ages making it through the mob back here. Besides, I'm dying for a drink."

"Me too," she agreed.

He took her arm and they made their way quickly up the stairs, well ahead of all the others. "I'm really sorry for what I said to Derek last night, Tori. I was out of order. Please forgive me. I don't know what gets into me at times."

"Forget it," she replied. "What's done is done. I need to get rid of this grease paint," she went on, still feeling a sense of letdown as she turned toward the make-up room. "See you in a few minutes. You're probably anxious to get out of that costume."

"You said it. This shirt collar seemed to get tighter every night."

"Well, you won't have to worry about it any more." Again, she experienced the strong sense of loss. "It's all over now," she added, as though trying to convince herself. All over with the play and all over with us.

Alone with her reflection, Victoria stood very still, aware of the post-play chatter coming from below yet feeling oddly detached from all of it. The play had gone well. She was certain Max would be pleased. Mitch had been incredibly co-operative for the last night. Everybody in the cast had been great. They'd moved and spoken together like a perfect, well-oiled machine. The roars of laughter and the standing ovation from the crowd had provided ample proof of their enjoyment of the comedy. Mitch had partially redeemed himself by making certain she got her fair share of the laughs for the closing night. He could be likable when he wanted to. She hope they could part amicably.

Tori dipped her fingers into a pot of cold cream and drew several white question marks on her forehead and cheeks. She'd better get a move on, she told herself, if she wanted to get cleaned up before the others arrived. She'd bought a slinky red dress for the party, and she could scarcely wait to get home, shower, and put it on. She was looking forward to seeing Mary Alice and Allen again. They must have made it a point to return from overseas in time to catch the final night. Allen was a real theatre nut. She was anxious to ask him what he thought of their performance. She wanted to ask them all about Ireland, too, she reflected, wiping off the cold cream. She and Mitch had never talked about where they'd go on their honeymoon. Just as well, since there wasn't going to be one. Honeymoon. The word had a quaint, old-fashioned sound to it. It must have been romantic in the old days when couples waited for marriage. Bashful brides in filmy negligees. Eager grooms in crisp new Paisley pajamas. Champagne cooling in a bucket by the bed.

"Victoria!"

She turned to see Mitch peeking around the doorway. Only his head was visible.

"What do you want?"

"Give me a hand with this zipper, will you? I think it's stuck."

When she went out to help him, she saw he was wearing nothing but his blue jeans. The zipper was down—and it was indecently obvious to see why he couldn't pull it up.

"Mitch, you fool," she scolded. "The others will be up here any minute. Quit showing off how well-endowed you are and go finish dressing."

Victoria couldn't keep from laughing as she wiped off the last of her stage make-up. Mitch could behave so outrageously! Ever since last night's blow-up when he'd insulted both Drew and Derek, the two of them had been getting along fairly well, although she had avoided any intimacy between them. It hadn't been difficult. Mitch had been able to think of nothing but the play. She hoped he wouldn't take it too hard when she called off their engagement. One thing was comforting. She no longer felt torn by any indecision. By tomorrow, they would both be free agents again.

25
Bella's Closing Night Party

BELLA FARTHINGTON'S THREE-STOREY MONSTER HOUSE in the north end of the city was lit up like a great red brick Christmas tree. The sound of loud conversation and even louder music greeted Victoria and Mitch as they approached the front door.

"Bella's a widow, a patron of community theatre, and one of the first life members," Mitch confided as they rang the doorbell. Max told me she's the richest woman in this town. Husband left her pots of money. Guess that's why she's supplying all the booze tonight. At most of these theatre parties you have to stand around in the kitchen so you can keep an eye on your own bottle. If you don't, the characters who brought a cheap bottle of plunk will drink all your expensive stuff."

Bella herself opened the door, bearing down on them like a gaudily painted overweight angel in diaphanous white chiffon. Diamonds glittered from her ears and fingers as she clasped them each in turn. "Dahlings!" she gushed. "Come in, come in. You were mahvellous tonight. Simply mahvellous. Look who's here, everybody!" she called out, ushering them into an already crowed living room. "Priss and the Professor. Isn't it just too mahvellous!"

Raised glasses and smiles were directed towards them from various corners of the large cornflower-blue and white room. A circular Persian rug in the centre blazed with color and all the furniture looked to Tori like expensive antiques.

"Just help yourselves, dahlings," Bella cooed. "I gave my maid the night off. There's a bar set up in the dining room and kitchen as well as the one down in the rec room. Lots of cheese and crackers and goodies

Tall Stuff

everywhere. We're using the entire house tonight, so feel free to roam. Some of us are going to have a séance in my bedroom on the third floor later on. Do join us if you're so inclined." She wagged a warning index finger. "But only if you're serious. We're going to try to contact my dear old Willard. 'Course if we do, he'll have a heart attack seeing how I'm spending his money. Willard was never one for levity. But then spirits can't have heart attacks, can they? Poor Willy. That's what did him in— a massive one when he was seventy-five."

The crimson lips continued to move in a never-ending torrent of words. At the first pause, Victoria and Mitch broke away and bolted for the nearest bar. They found Max there, resplendent in black leather pants and a purple shirt. "Victoria!" he exclaimed. "You look sensational in red. Love the high heels! You look like a tall sexy bottle of ketchup."

Tori laughed. "I'd better have a drink before I respond to that. Where's Gloria?"

"Alas, Gloria has departed for greener fields. You'll never guess who she came with tonight."

"I doubt if it's her husband," Mitch remarked, handing Tori a light rum and Coke. She accepted it even though she preferred 7 Up as a mix.

Max chuckled. "Not bloody likely. She's with Neil Williams. He's been chosen to direct the next play. I guess Gloria's queer for directors."

"Speaking of queer," said Mitch, "look what just walked in."

"God, I hope Derek stays away tonight like he threatened," Max replied. "I don't think he could take this."

The new friend Bryan had in tow would have stood out in any group and even in this colorful crowd his startling appearance caused a minor sensation. For a moment, conversation ceased as everyone stared. The boy looked to be in his late teens. He was tall and lithe with pale blonde hair that curled under just as it touched the collar of his indigo silk shirt. His black leather jeans were so tight they looked as though they'd been painted on. Tori wondered whether his hair had been bleached. Its platinum sheen made a striking contrast with his large violet-colored eyes. Three golden hoops dangled from one of his ears. A blue fish tattoo decorated his neck. He wore half a dozen gold chains and an equal number of rings.

"This is Bradley, everybody," Bryan sang out. "Don't our names go well together? Bee and Bee."

"Bee for bullshit," Max mumbled.

Poor Derek, Tori thought. Derek with his bad breath and desperate neediness. He wouldn't stand a chance with young Bradley around. Well, she'd been right about one thing. Bryan had shown up for the party as she'd assured Derek he would. She hoped Derek would stick to his decision to stay away as he'd threatened. She'd grown fond of him and hated to see him hurt. Forcing her mind away from the subject, she turned to Max. "Have you seen Allen and Mary Alice yet?" she asked.

"They're talking to some of the Frosty Prosties in Bella's greenhouse. Grab another drink and I'll show you two where it is."

"Okay. Coming, Mitch?"

"I'll catch up with you later. I want to mingle for awhile."

"Probably wants to mingle with the next director," Max whispered in her ear.

They watched, amused, as Mitch took off in the direction of Gloria and her new love, Neil Williams.

"He's probably already thinking about his next starring role," Max observed, grinning as he led her through the noisy house along the blue carpeted hallway towards the back door. "He seems to think he has a future in the theatre, a professional one."

Victoria turned to glance at the director's finely-chiseled features. His was such a poker face she couldn't decide whether he looked unhappy or not. "I'm sorry about Gloria," she said. "The way things turned out, I mean."

He shrugged. "It's just as well, Tori. She was getting too possessive by far. She'd even started hinting she'd get a divorce if I wanted. But I put too much value on my freedom to get sucked into anything like that."

"I've had my so-called freedom for several years now, Max, and frankly I don't see anything so great about it."

Max chuckled. "That's because basically you women are all the same. You all want a couple of kids and a vine-covered cottage – whether you admit it or not."

"I admit it. That definitely doesn't hold true for all women though.

Lots of them are happily single. But I have noticed one thing. For all their yakking about freedom, single people, both men and women, don't seem to be one bit happier than married ones."

At the rear of the mansion, they turned into a sanctuary so lovely Tori stood stock still and stared. Daffodils, irises, hyacinths, and tulips were blooming everywhere. Water cascaded gently from a cupid-encrusted fountain in one corner of the greenhouse. Beside it, Allen and Mary Alice were snuggled together in a white wicker love seat. They rose as one when Max and Tori joined them, embracing in a shower of greetings and congratulations.

"Prosties gone?" asked Max.

"Debbie decided she was ready to stand on her head," Allen said, laughing. "You know her—she needs a good-sized audience for that."

"It's so pretty out here," said Mary Alice. "We were going to sit here a few minutes longer before looking for you, Tori."

"Where's Mitch?" asked Allen. " I hear you two are an item. Didn't you come together?"

"Mitch is a good mixer at parties. Just like Coke," she joked. I probably won't see him for hours." Even as she said the words, she found herself hoping they wouldn't come true. Even though she'd finally decided to call it quits, she didn't want to look neglected. She didn't want people feeling sorry for her. She wanted their last night together to end on a happy note. Tomorrow she'd give him back his ring. "Tell me all about Ireland," she said as Max left them. "I'll bet it's something to see."

Within short minutes Tori found herself transported to a land of leprechauns and race horses, a land a hundred shades of green with singing pubs where strangers became friends and stayed that way till closing time.

"We hated to leave the auld sod," said Allen.

"He's not referring to his great-uncle," Mary Alice teased.

"He's a great guy as well as a great- uncle," Allen went on. "He couldn't do enough for us in the way of hospitality. Drove us all over the place. We saw the beautiful scenery where they made an old film called Ryan's Daughter. At least I think that's what it was called."

"The coastline there is gorgeous," Mary Alice agreed.

"It all sounds fascinating," Tori said. "I'd love to visit Ireland myself some day."

Mary Alice giggled. "Nothing's much fun by yourself, Tori. Where's that man of yours?"

Victoria could feel color rising in her cheeks. Mary Alice could still irritate her at times. But she knew in her heart the remark hadn't been a barbed one. Forcing a smile, she rose. "I'm going to get another drink. See you later."

On her way back to the house a short man stopped and stared her up and down. "Wow!" he exclaimed, looking surprised. "You look like a Globetrotter. Do you play basketball?" he asked, slurring his words.

"No, I don't," she replied. "Do you play miniature golf?"

He ignored the question and staggered away.

Chalk one up for me, she thought, pleased with her retort though he was probably too drunk to get it.

The entire place was now jammed to the rafters with hordes of gaudy, chattering partiers, many people Tori had never seen before. Bella must have invited everyone even remotely connected with community theatre, she decided. As she entered, she saw a noisy group heading for the stairs. Derek was with them. He seemed very drunk, but his face had a stricken look. Damn Bryan anyway, she thought. Damn all people who hurt other people. You might want to end an affair, but you don't have to be cruel about it. She was suddenly so anxious for another drink she shoved her way towards the bar in the kitchen. As she did so, a buxom redhead turned and frowned at her. Tori was wondering where she'd seen the woman before when a youth who looked young enough to be her son ordered her to get a move on. Tori noticed he was wearing a tee shirt with the words THE ILLEGAL SMILE printed beneath a goofy looking face. The redhead handed him his drink and the two walked off, arm in arm. Tori turned back to the bar. A shirt like that would make a perfect gift for Mitch, she reflected. She hoped he wasn't overdoing the drinking or the smoking up—wherever he was. All at once she heard a familiar voice at her elbow.

"Can I fix you a drink?"

"Drew! I didn't expect to see you here."

"Why not?"

Tall Stuff

"Well, I had the idea, forgive me if I'm wrong, that you didn't much like theatre people."

"You're wrong. But I forgive you."

"But..."

"Look, Tori, we can't talk here. Too noisy. And far too crowded. Come upstairs with me and I'll tell you what it is I do like and admire about them."

She hesitated. Why did she always feel a little nervous around Andrew Macdonald? Nervous and excited at the same time. She glanced quickly around. Mitch was nowhere to be seen. Why not have a quiet drink with Drew, she decided. She enjoyed his company.

"I'll freshen your drink," he said. "Rum and 7 Up. Right"

She was touched he remembered. That was more than Mitch had done earlier. "Make it a double," she said. "By the looks of everyone here, I've got some catching up to do."

Glasses held aloft, they made their way up to the second floor. "This looks fine," remarked Drew, opening to door to one of the bedrooms on their left. They padded across the thick rug to the wide bed. Drew reached down to push back a pile of coats so they could sit there. They both jumped when the pile of coats began to move—seemingly of its own accord.

"Sorry," Drew stammered as he and Tori choked back irreverent laughter.

They retreated hastily from the dimly lit room and proceeded along the hall till they came to a small study that was clearly unoccupied.

"That's the part I don't like," said Drew. "God, they're so damn promiscuous. It's incredible."

"Maybe they can't help it...the ones who are like that," Tori protested. "Nobody has a right to judge. I used to feel the same way as you, but maybe we take all this sex stuff too seriously."

"You're right. We really shouldn't sit in judgment. I'll tell you one thing, though. When I get married, it's going to be a one to one relationship. And it's going to be for keeps. I think I told you before, I was with someone for quite awhile, and I thought it was going somewhere. Then I found out she didn't want kids. Ever. I had already bought a house with a backyard in anticipation of having a family. So we went our separate ways."

Victoria said nothing. He could have been putting her own dream into words, she reflected.

"Let's sit here," shall we? He indicated a comfortable looking brown settee.

Tori looked around. The only other furnishing in the room consisted of a large mahogany desk and chair, a low, glass-topped coffee table, and a couple of large potted plants. She took a sip of her drink and sat down beside him, overwhelmingly conscious of his physical presence until they started talking.

"The productions are always worth seeing," Drew said, "and this one was certainly no exception. After all amateur just means love, not amateurish or inferior. It makes me mad sometimes. People will travel hundreds of miles and spend hundreds of dollars to see professional theatre, but they won't go across the street to see local talent. Sunfield's getting better, though. Crowds have been pretty good for the past couple of seasons. Are you going to read for the next play, Tori?"

The question surprised her. She hadn't given any thought whatsoever to any further acting. She'd only gone into it in the first place to get close to Mitch Ames. What a fiasco that had turned out to be! She could hardly wait to see the last of him. She'd have to go home with him tonight, but that would be the end of it. Tomorrow he'd get his ring back. It had never been a good fit—not in any way.

"Tori?"

"Sorry. I was daydreaming."

"You didn't answer my question. About acting again. Just for the record, I think you're very good."

"Thanks, Drew. That means a lot, coming from you." She stared at the abstract painting of a nude above the desk. "I'm not really interested in acting though. Or maybe the word I'm looking for is dedicated. I resent giving up so much of my free time."

"Their absolute dedication is what I most admire about community theatre people," said Andrew. "I once knew a fellow who got a bad cut in a sword fight in Roshomon. He stayed with it though—finished the play before he went to the hospital. Had to have half a dozen stitches to close the wound. Then there was another actor who had to play the harmonium with a broken thumb in Flint. It was a Festival entry and he didn't want to let the other players down."

"I know what you mean," said Tori. "And it's not just the performers who give their all. Look at the way the backstage crew works. They were probably there for hours dismantling that set after everybody else left tonight. The actors get a lot of glory—for a few nights, anyway. But what do the backstage people get out of it?"

"They do it for love alone. It's important for everybody to have a passion for something. Doesn't much matter what it is—cooking, creative writing, weaving, painting, pottery—the list is endless. With me, it's my job at the paper—even though some days I'd like to throw my computer through the window."

Tori smiled and set her drink on the coffee table. She felt happy and relaxed, enjoying talking with Drew, liking the sound of his voice with its slight Scottish burr.

All at once, Drew took her left hand and held it up. "I see you're still wearing the ring. No—don't stop me from saying this." His words poured forth in a rush. "I have to tell you something. I've fallen in love with you, Victoria. I know I shouldn't have, but I just wanted you to know that I have. Even though I know it's too late, I love everything about you."

She opened her mouth to tell him the truth just as Mitch came charging into the room. One look at him and she knew he was very drunk. His brown eyes were glazed, his usually neat hair was in wild disorder, and his mouth was smeared with various shades of lipstick.

"On your feet, Macdonald!" he roared, slurring the words almost beyond recognition. "Itch high time I straightened you out."

Tori's nervous laughter seemed to galvanize Mitch into further action. He rushed forward, grabbed Andrew's shirt with one hand, and jammed the knuckles of his other hand into the journalist's face.

In a flash, Drew was on his feet. "I don't want to fight you, Ames," he began, but when his drunken opponent tried to punch him, Andrew's fist shot out. Someone by the door screamed.

Mitch looked up at both of them from the floor, one hand clutching his mouth. "If you broke my nose I'll shoe you!" he threatened, his words a mumbled jumble.

Everything had happened so fast Tori felt dazed, unable to move. But when she saw a red trickle of blood appear between Mitch's fingers, she rushed to his side. "Drew, you shouldn't have. Mitch was in no condition to defend himself."

Andrew glared down at her. "Love isn't only blind in your case, Tori. It's deaf and dumb as well."

"How dare you!" she protested. "You've no right to judge me—especially after hitting a drunk man, a man incapable of defending himself…" But Andrew was already turning to make his way through the crowd of curious onlookers gathered in the open doorway.

"Quiet down there!" a female voice shrilled above the confusion. "Bella's trying to hold a séance up here."

Tori shuddered with revulsion as Mitch reached up to grab her, pulling her to the floor alongside him. Her new red dress was stained now with blood. Lucky it was red, she thought, not knowing whether to laugh or cry. "Show's over," she called to the few remaining faces in the doorway. "I've got to get this guy home."

With Max's help, she loaded Mitch into his car and talked him out of the keys so she could drive. The director tried to make a joke of it, but Tori was far closer to tears than she was to laughter. She kept seeing the look on Andrew's face as he left. If only she'd had a chance to explain, tell him she was no longer engaged.

26
Regret For What Might Have Been

AFTER SEEING MITCH SAFELY INTO HIS APARTMENT and dumping him unceremoniously onto his bed, Tori was sitting in her kitchen drinking a lot of coffee and doing a lot of regretting. She hadn't even bothered to remove his shoes. Let him be uncomfortable, the liar. Just as she was unlocking his door she'd remembered where she'd seen the buxom redhead from the party. An unsavory looking character if ever there was one. She was the same woman Tori had once seen opening Mitch's door with her own key. The woman he'd said was his cleaning lady. Not that she'd ever bought that story in the first place. She'd wanted to believe it at the time. Maybe that was why she'd accepted his explanation without question. People generally believed what they wanted to believe. And after a few of Mitch's passionate kisses she'd been ready to forget everything but her need for him. What you don't know can't hurt you—unless you rip away the wool from your own eyes and see reality for what it is. She was seeing it now—and she didn't like what she saw. She'd been such a fool for such a long time! The one thing she was relieved about was the fact she'd always insisted he used protection—even at their most ardent moments together, even when he'd protested that since she was on the pill and they were engaged there was no need for it. Like making love with gloves on, he'd called it.

As the first rays of daylight came slanting in through her yellow kitchen curtains, Tori's thoughts turned to Andrew Macdonald's rushed declaration of love .She kept seeing his half-eager, half-shy smile. Kept recalling the way a series of small laugh lines fanned out from the corners of his clear blue eyes. She was at least two inches taller than him, but her height didn't seem to matter—to either of them. She remembered dancing with him—and how right it had felt. She knew now why she'd always been a little nervous around him. She loved him, too. She wished she'd had time to tell him she was ending her engagement to Mitch. What a mess she'd made of everything! Drew would probably never want to see her again. If only she hadn't been so upset by the sight of Mitch's blood. If only she hadn't felt an obligation to see him safely home. She recalled Drew's last words to her. "Love isn't only blind in your case, Tori. It's deaf and dumb as well."

Cruel words, but she couldn't deny their truth. She shouldn't have shouted at Drew the way she had. It must have been the fighting that set her off. She'd been afraid Mitch's injury was serious, though it had proven to be nothing more than a nosebleed. He'd asked for worse than that, charging at Drew like a madman. Small wonder Andrew's first instinct was to strike back. She was certain it was the unflattering review rather than jealousy that had precipitated Mitch's attack.

She'd behaved like a complete idiot. She had indeed been deaf, dumb, and blind. She deserved the contempt Andrew must surely feel for her now. She would finish with Mitch today, she decided, even if he was suffering the mother of all hangovers.

Tori rose, set her empty coffee mug in the sink, and went into the bathroom. For a few moments she stood there, quietly turning her hated diamond back and forth. It had never been the right size. She'd been blinded by sheer animal attraction—along with a burning desire for the stability of marriage. She held her left hand under a stream of cold water, and using a little face soap, worked the ring around her finger until she was able to slip it off. She tossed it on the counter, and after closing her drapes against the late autumn sunrise, kicked off her high heels, pulled off her red silk dress and crawled miserably into bed.

27
Showdown Time

AT ONE-THIRTY IN THE AFTERNOON TORI WOKE to the sound of someone pounding loudly on her door. She rubbed her eyes, feeling slightly disoriented as she looked around her darkened bedroom. Then she caught sight of her new red dress lying in a crumpled heap on the floor, and the whole disastrous evening came back to her. She rose, pulled on her brown and gold robe, and went reluctantly to answer the knocking, which was growing in intensity.

"All right, dammit, I'm coming," she grumbled, automatically tidying her hair with one hand as she looked through the tiny peephole to see who was there. Then she pulled open the door.

Mitch stood before her, not saying a word. For long seconds they simply stared at each other.

"May I come in?" he asked, his voice controlled, cold and aloof.

His appearance caught Tori off guard. She had expected a contrite, apologetic, and miserably hung over Mitch, not this well-groomed, formally dressed stranger.

"You've shaved off your mustache," she said.

"Tell me something I don't know," he replied, aping her remark about the cold sore.

"Don't worry—I intend to," she replied curtly. "But you'll have to excuse me for a few minutes. I just woke up. Sit down and grab a magazine or something. I'll be right back."

Tori studied her face in the mirror above the bathroom sink. She looked a mess. Mascara had formed dark circles under her eyes, making her pale complexion look stark white by comparison. Her mouth felt as though she'd been chewing cotton batting. Hurriedly, she splashed cold water over her face and brushed her teeth and hair. She was about to join Mitch when she turned back to the mirror to apply a touch of pink to her lips and cheeks. They were going to have a showdown, and a showdown was no time to be caught looking less than her best. She thought briefly about getting dressed but decided she didn't have time. Besides, the robe she was wearing was still attractive. It was one she'd worn to make herself pretty for Mitch after one of their early dates. Not so long ago, really, but it seemed half a lifetime to her now. Such a lot had happened since then. Mary Alice's marriage, the play, her engagement to Mitch—an engagement that had been precipitated by his jealousy of her brother Billy. She'd never gotten around to telling him about her brother's visit. So Mitch wasn't the only one who'd been dishonest, she reflected. Their whole relationship had been based on dishonesty, some of it hers. Like going after the role of Priss in the play.

For the second time, she turned back to the sink. The small diamond lay sparkling beside the white porcelain soap dish. She picked it up and carried it with her into the living room. Mitch was seated stiffly in one corner of the white velour sofa. He turned when she entered.

"You were gone so long I thought you'd gone back to bed," he complained.

Tori sat down at the other end of the sofa. "I was doing a little thinking," she said. "About us."

He glanced down at the ring in the palm of her hand, but his chocolate brown eyes betrayed not the slightest hint of curiosity.

"Actually, I've been doing a lot of thinking about us," she went on.

"And did you reach any earth-shattering conclusions?"

"I did," she replied.

"Would you care to share them with me?" His tone was acidic.

"Nobody can share anything with you, Mitch, because you don't know the meaning of the word. You've never given me any emotional support when I needed it. You wouldn't even come with me to my godchild's first birthday party."

"Why should I go where I'm not wanted. Your friend Kate doesn't like me. I don't like her either, for that matter. And I don't like kids birthday parties."

"You don't like kids. Period."

"I didn't say that. Look, Tori, I didn't come over here to engage in any deep psychological discussion about my deplorable character. I came to ask what in hell you were doing last night alone in an upstairs bedroom with Andrew Macdonald."

He was so transparent Tori felt like laughing. The old 'take the defensive' ploy. Get mad first.

"It won't work, Mitch."

He pretended ignorance. "What won't work?"

"Your little game. Trying to put me in the wrong. You're the one who got drunk, who had lipstick smeared all over his face, who started a fight..."

"Over you."

"Crap. Or, as Max would say, bee for bullshit."

Mitch fumbled for a cigarette. It took him a few minutes to regain his composure. "You don't mind if I break your no smoking rule just this once, do you?"

She rose to hunt up a saucer he could use for an ashtray. "You've been itching to slug Drew ever since his review on you in Banana Boats," she accused.

"That isn't true."

"The hell it isn't."

He lit the cigarette and took a long drag before replying. "You still haven't explained why you were upstairs alone with him in a bedroom."

"It was a study. And we were just talking."

"Talking. Ha! That's a laugh!"

"Don't judge everybody by yourself, Mitch. Oh, by the way, I saw your cleaning lady at the party."

"My what?"

"You know—that titian-haired gal with the forty-eight inch bust. I guess she found someone younger than you to work for, eh?"

The last of Mitch's cool exterior melted away. "Oh, for god's sake, Tori, let's not get into that again. That's all water under the bridge."

"Who cleans your stove now? Or hauls your ashes? Tell me, Mitch, does she do windows? Maybe I could use her once a week."

"Tori, if you must know, I was getting a little hash from her now and then."

"You were getting a little something, all right." Tori sighed and sat down again. "Mitch, let's stop this. It really doesn't matter to me any more. It's time we called it quits. You're not ready for marriage. You've been evasive with me too many times. And to tell you the truth, I haven't been exactly honest with you. That was my brother Billy you saw me with the weekend before you proposed. I always meant to tell you, but somehow I never got around to it."

For a moment, he looked surprised. But he recovered quickly. "I don't care about that, Tori. I still want to marry you. As far as that redhead goes, she meant less than nothing to me."

"Mitch, I don't want any explanations. We made a mistake. Let's just forget the whole thing."

"You know you don't mean that."

"Oh, but I do. Believe me."

He continued to smoke, watching her with narrowed eyes. "Just because I had a little side action. After all, we're not married yet."

"Mitch, I told you. I don't care about that. I've felt for some time now we're all wrong for each other. We don't want the same things out of life."

"I want you, Tori. I'm crazy about you. You know that." He butted his cigarette and moved closer to her. "Kiss me and tell me you don't love me," he said, trying to take her in his arms.

Firmly, she pushed him away. "Not this time, Mitch. We can't solve our problems that way any more. What we had physically was good, but not good enough to hold a marriage together. We're not...we're not friends, Mitch. You don't really know me at all. You've never asked me anything about my family. Or told me much about yours. We have to call it off."

"But everyone knows we're engaged. What'll we tell people?"

"Who cares? That's not important. It's our lives we're talking about here. It doesn't have anything to do with anybody else."

Murmuring her name, he reached for her again, but she struggled free and rose trembling to her feet. "Don't make this harder than it has to be." She leaned down and picked up the diamond ring. "Here. I'm sorry. I'm truly sorry it has to end this way."

"But it doesn't have to end, Tori. Don't do this to us. Put the ring on and come here."

Tall Stuff

Mitch had assumed his 'little boy lost' look. It was his most appealing expression, and Tori had always responded warmly to it in the past. She was totally immune to it now.

He brushed a lock of wavy brown hair away from his dark eyes and looked up at her, his handsome features infinitely sad. "I can't believe you mean what you're saying, Tori. I can't believe it's all over between us."

"You'll have to accept it, Mitch." She dropped the ring into the breast pocket of his silky beige suit coat. "You'd better leave now. There's nothing more to be said."

His lost expression was rapidly changing to one of anger as he rose. "Maybe there's nothing more to be said," he muttered, "but there sure as hell is something more to be done."

Pushing her aside, he strode to the door of her apartment and slammed it soundly behind him.

For a long time after Mitch left, Tori stood very still, staring at the familiar objects around her as though seeing them for the first time: the amber paperweight on the coffee table her sister Rita had given her on a long-ago birthday, the pewter mug she'd brought back as a souvenir from San Francisco, the colorful paper flowers Mary Alice had fashioned last Easter, the hand-carved candle holder her brother Billy had made when he was sixteen. As her eyes moved from one object to another, Mitch's final words echoed in her head. "There sure as hell is something more to be done."

She knew only too well what he would do. Go out and get as stoned as possible as fast as possible. Be that as it may, she thought, there was nothing she could do about it. Mitch was weak. Mary Alice had once said something about his being dangerous. Tori smiled at the thought. He was dangerous, all right. Dangerous to overly romantic, gullible girls like she'd been.

Feeling totally exhausted, Tori collapsed on the sofa, leaned back and closed her eyes. She was glad she'd had the strength to follow through on her decision. But even though she was relieved it was over, she felt unbearably alone. She'd be glad to go back to work on Monday. Hospitals were always busy places. It would help take her mind off herself—for several hours of the day at least. It was the other hours she was worried about. She shouldn't have reacted so strongly against Drew. He'd probably never want to see her again.

28
Tori Tells All to Millie

ALTHOUGH IT WAS ALWAYS HECTIC IN EMERGENCY, getting back to work didn't help as much as Tori hoped it would. She seemed to be existing in a kind of limbo, unable to make any definite decisions about personal affairs that had to be seen to—and soon. Her father was looking forward to walking her down the aisle; her stepmother and Rita were looking forward to a wedding—as mother of the bride and matron-of-honor

Several times she'd tried to force herself to pick up the telephone, call them, and tell them the wedding was off, but each time she'd begun to call a lump formed in her throat and she'd been afraid she'd break down and cry. That was the last thing she wanted to do. She'd have to put it off for a couple of weeks, she decided. Give herself time to get used to the idea. Her father had been so pleased she was finally "settling down" as he called it. The news was going to break his heart. He was old-fashioned enough to use the term "old maid". Tori had a hunch he harbored a secret fear she was going to be one. She was all for matrimony herself, but she wouldn't get married just for the sake of being married—not if she had to stay single all her life. The wrong husband would be infinitely worse than no husband at all. Lots of cases of so-called wedded bliss she saw were anything but blissful. Few people were as lucky as her best friend Kate in finding a soul mate. Or her friend Millie at the hospital. If only she hadn't spoiled everything with Andrew.

Tori realized she'd begun to neglect her appearance, but somehow she couldn't bring herself to take any real interest in how she looked.

Her black hair grew lank and oily for lack of washing, her complexion dry for lack of moisturizing lotion. So far she'd managed to avoid running into Mitch, but she was aware she'd have to move if she wanted to steer clear of him forever. In any case, the large apartment was too expensive for her to keep up alone for much longer. Though she couldn't yet bring herself to look in the want ads for new living quarters. Aside from reading Andrew's Town Talk column and staring for long moments at his picture, she ignored the daily paper.

Mary Alice and Allen called twice to invite her over, but Tori put them off with vague excuses, afraid their happiness would only make her feel worse by comparison. People tried but failed to cheer her up. It was as though the real Tori had fled and a disagreeable stranger had taken her place. Millie told her as much on her fifth day back at work.

"What's wrong, Tori?" she asked. "Your face gets any longer, you're going to trip over it. Maybe talking will help. No-come on. Don't rush off this time. Come and have a coffee with me before you head for home. It may not help, but what can it hurt?"

Silently Victoria followed her to the cafeteria. They were seated at a table by the window before she broke the silence. "Oh, Millie, I'm so miserable I could die. I was so sure I was in love with Mitch Ames. How could I have been so stupid!"

The older woman reached for Tori's left hand and held it gently for a moment before removing her own. "You broke your engagement?"

"Yes. But I'm not unhappy about that. Not a bit. Mitch was all wrong for me. I know that now."

Millie took a mint from her ever-present supply. "Mitch Ames? The fellow who played the part of the professor in Banana Boats at Midnight?"

"None other."

"You were engaged to him?"

"Why so surprised?"

Thoughtfully Millie sipped her coffee. "I know I shouldn't judge by first impressions," she said finally, "but I met him backstage after the play and it seemed to me he was too much in love with himself to ever fall for anybody else."

Tori came closer to laughing than she had for days. "He is," she agreed, "and I think it's one affair that's going to last for a lifetime."

"How did you get involved with him?"

Tori leaned on one elbow. "I don't know, Millie. I was completely obsessed with him from the day he moved into my apartment building. He was so tall—and so darned good-looking. I suppose it was a case of lust at first sight."

Millie chuckled. "Okay, so if you're not sorry about giving him back the Hope diamond, what is wrong?"

Tori was surprised to find herself putting thoughts into words, thoughts she hadn't truly faced up to until this moment. "I believe I really am in love with someone now. His name is Andrew Macdonald. He writes the Town Talk columns. I've been reading them so long I feel as though I've known him for years. I've seen him a few times, and we really seem to connect. It's all such a mess!"

"What do you mean? What's a mess? If you're really in love this time, that's good, isn't it?"

Tori sighed and cupped her chin in both hands. "I ruined any chance I might have had with Drew," she replied, her voice scarcely more than a whisper. "I behaved like a fool the last time we were together. Mitch got drunk and picked a fight with him at Bella Farthington's party. I told Drew off for fighting back. I shouldn't have. He was just defending himself. I'm sure he despises me now, and I don't blame him if he does."

"Can't you see him...talk to him...explain why you behaved the way you did."

Tori shook her head. "I can't, Millie. I couldn't face him." She paused. "I do feel better now, though. It was good to talk to you. It always is. You're a real friend. Thanks for listening."

The older woman finished the last of her peppermint. "We'd better call it a day, kid. But think it over—about talking to this Drew fellow, I mean. Sometimes the simplest things in life seem like the most difficult."

29
In The Doldrums of Bad Dreams

AFTER HER REVELATION to Millie, Tori spent a restless night thinking long thoughts about Andrew Macdonald. He certainly wasn't handsome in the way Mitch was. But physical attraction was something like inherited money—nice to have, but not particularly admirable in itself. Besides, she liked Andrew's face. It was amiable and rugged—and lit by an intelligence worth far more than mere good looks. So what if he wasn't as tall as she? Tori recalled dancing with him, and height was the last thing she'd been thinking of. Those worries were behind her; teenage days when she'd felt like an Amazon with every partner brave enough to haul her out onto the floor. She hadn't lacked for partners once her high school days were over. Lots of short men liked to prove themselves capable of attracting tall girls. Tori smiled, remembering some of the short men who'd chatted her up—men who wouldn't have appealed to her even if they'd been six feet tall.

Like a flock of homing pigeons, her thoughts kept returning to Drew. Could she really be in love with a man she'd never even kissed? Yes, she decided, she could. She'd not only danced with him, she'd shared serious conversations as well as irreverent laughter. They were on the same wavelength. She was certain of that. The only disagreements they'd had involved Mitch. Maybe she hadn't spent a lot of time with Drew, but it was quality not quantity that mattered. He'd tried to tell her from the beginning that Mitch was all wrong for her, but she'd been too infatuated to listen. Her passion for Mitch had been hot, all right. So hot she'd been badly burned. She'd behaved like an idiot. There was no way she could face Andrew after the scene at Bella's party.

Tall Stuff

When finally she fell asleep, Tori had a strange and disturbing dream. She was alone on a huge stage, row upon row of empty seats facing her. The deserted theatre seemed to be an open-air one, yet everything was in darkness—not totally black but in varying shades of grey. The air was very still, no sound save that of her own labored breathing. As her eyes swept across the rows of empty seats, they slowly began to fill, until hundreds of black shapes seemed to be staring up at her. She could feel a sea of eyes riveted on her body, although she couldn't make out any faces. All at once she was caught in a beam of while light, like the searchlight of an airport. Heart thundering, she raced from one side of the vast stage to the other, trying to avoid the cruel light. It was useless. She kept getting caught in its unrelenting glare. Hyena-like laughter from the crowd rolled over her like waves from a deep, black ocean. She looked down and saw to her horror she was stark naked.

Tori awoke, clutching blankets and sheets as beads of perspiration prickled her forehead. She groped blindly for the light switch on the night lamp beside her bed. It wasn't until the room was bathed in its soft yellow glow that she was able to breathe easily again. She rose, heated some milk, and took the mug back to bed with her. The hot drink comforted her a little, but it was a long time before she was able to fall asleep once more.

30
The Walking Wounded in Emergency

NEXT DAY THERE WERE DARK CIRCLES UNDER TORI'S EYES as she attended to her duties in Emergency Admitting. She'd tried to cover them with liquid make-up, but her attempts at camouflage had been singularly unsuccessful. The weird dream continued to haunt her as she moved robot-like through her morning routine.

Emergency was even busier than usual with its assortment of walking wounded: a middle-aged woman complaining of violent headaches, a young truck driver with a deep cut on his right thumb, a mother with a toddler who'd taken a bad fall, a teenager suffering from burns on both hands. The parade of human misery went on and on until Tori felt ready to scream. But she gritted her teeth and soldiered on, trying to shut personal problems out of her mind. Just before lunch, a man rapped on the counter before her window, seeking attention. She looked up, surprised. Andrew Macdonald stood facing her.

"Drew!" she exclaimed. "What are you doing here?"

He seemed as shocked to see her as she was to see him. Several seconds passed before he spoke. Somewhere a child cried loudly for his mother.

"Is something wrong?" she asked.

"I don't know for certain," he replied, the Scottish burr more noticeable than usual in his voice. "I think I might have a broken arm."

"What happened?"

He paused, looking concerned. "I got shoved, sort of. To tell the truth, I'd rather not go into it. All I want to do is get an x-ray. My arm might only be bruised, but I'd like to make sure."

Tall Stuff

"Have you called your doctor?"

"Aye. It happened right in front of the newspaper office, so I went back in and called him from there. He said he'd be here as soon as he could make it."

Tori led him into a room across the way where a clerk sat waiting in front of a computer. "She'll need a little information, Drew."

Drew looked uncomfortable.

"Just your health card and address," Tori went on.

"All right then. Let's get on with it."

His voice held an edge of steel as he gave the required information to the young clerk. Tori wanted to tell him she was sorry he'd been hurt, but his face had a cold, set look that precluded further conversation between them.

"I hope everything's okay," she called as he followed another nurse along the corridor towards the x-ray department. He turned and looked back at her with a strange expression in his blue eyes, but he made no reply.

Even though it was fifteen minutes into Tori's lunch hour, she didn't want to go to the cafeteria for fear of missing Drew when he came back. He'd looked at her in such a peculiar way—almost as though it was her fault he'd been hurt. But not really accusing, either. More an expression of regret. When he returned, she made up her mind, she'd try to talk to him, tell him her engagement to Mitch was over. If he was no longer interested, well that was a chance she'd have to take.

But Andrew didn't come back. Dozens of people passed in and out of the swinging glass doors, but he was never one of them. Finally, Tori could stand the suspense no longer. She rushed along the corridor to the x-ray department.

"Andrew Macdonald," she said to the technician, a man she knew only as 'Bud'. "He came here to see if his arm was broken."

"Tell you in a minute," replied Bud.

Tori closed her eyes and crossed her fingers for luck.

"Nope. No broken bones," replied the technician. "But he left at least half an hour ago. You must have missed each other."

Tori's shoulders sagged, and a lump rose painfully in her throat.

"Yes," she said slowly. "I guess we missed each other."

Throat constricting and tears threatening, Tori retraced her steps. Drew must have left by another exit to avoid seeing her. If she'd had any doubt about his feelings toward her before, she now knew for certain he really wanted nothing more to do with her.

31
It's Not Always a Sin to Tell a Lie

MITCH WAS WAITING OUTSIDE HER DOOR when Tori returned from the hospital at three-thirty. He looked more than a little drunk—and more than a little pleased with himself.

"What are you doing here?" she demanded. Then, because she could think of nothing else to say to break the silence, she asked, "How come you're not at work?"

"Took the day off," he drawled, slurring the words. "Had some special work to do. Gave your journalist friend a little scare—one he won't forget in a hurry."

Tori gasped. "So you're responsible for Drew's injury! That's why he didn't want to say anything to me at the hospital." She stopped, unwilling to share the thought of finishing the sentence aloud. It was such a good thought she wanted to hold it close to her like a precious secret. Drew did still care about her—cared so much he hadn't wanted to hurt her by making accusations against the man he thought to be her fiancé. If only she'd had a chance to talk to him, to explain she was no longer involved with Mitch Ames.

Mitch was staring at her with a curious expression. He appeared to be struggling through an alcoholic haze to make sense out of what she was saying. The smell of whiskey was so strong it seemed to be coming from his very pores. How could she have ever deluded herself into thinking she loved him? She would talk to Andrew, she decided. It wasn't too late. There was no point in standing on false pride waiting for him to make the first move. But right now she had to deal with the immediate problem of Mitch.

"If you don't mind," she said coldly, "I'd like to go into my apartment. Please get out of my way."

"Florence Nightingale in tight white pants," he joked, his expression changing from a sneer to one of open hostility.

A tremor of fear passed through her as she dug her key out of her purse. Maybe her roommate had been right in calling him dangerous. "Please stand aside, Mitch. I'm tired and I want to lie down."

He remained where he was, hands in pockets as he leaned against her door. "I'll lie down with you," he suggested.

"I want to go in now. Alone."

"Don't you want to hear what happened?"

"I know what happened. You got into some kind of fight with Drew."

"I scared the shit out of him. Zipped by on my bike just as he was leaving the Sunfield Times and going for his car. Christ, you should have seen him jump!"

Drew must have bumped his arm against his car door, Tori reflected. What an idiotic stunt for a grown man like Mitch to pull! But then Mitch wasn't really a man. He was more like a spoiled little boy. She decided he needed to be taught a lesson. One he wouldn't forget.

"You did more than just scare Andrew Macdonald, Mitch," she said. "He's seriously injured. He hit his head on the curb when he fell. I was on duty at the hospital when they brought him in. He was unconscious when I left. Either you get the hell out of my way right now or I'll see to it that he presses charges against you. I'll even go to court to testify on his behalf."

The lie was far from being a white one, but Tori felt no remorse—not even when she saw that Mitch had turned very pale.

"I only meant to scare him," he mumbled, moving out of her way.

"You don't use a motorcycle to scare people. Not if you have any brains at all."

"Tori, I'm sorry. I'm sorry about everything that's happened. I miss you so much. I need you. I've been going crazy without you. Can't we try again?"

"No," she replied, fitting her key into the lock. "We can't."

"It's Macdonald, isn't it? He's the reason you dumped me."

Tall Stuff

She tried to remain calm, but she was shaking. "How I feel about Drew is no concern of yours."

"It does concern me, Tori." He tried to take her hand, but she pulled it away. "It concerns me because if he likes you, he'll do whatever you say. You can talk to him. Tell him I didn't intend to hurt him or anything. Christ, it happened right in front of the Sunfield Times. Any witnesses there would be sure to be on his side."

Tori looked at his pretty, pouting face and marveled afresh at how she could ever have fallen for so cowardly a man. "I'll see what I can do," she replied with a saccharine smile. "But only if you stay away from me from now on. I mean that. I never want to see you again."

Once inside her apartment, Tori went directly to the telephone. She'd try the paper first, she decided. If Drew wasn't there, she'd get his home number from them. Tell them it was an emergency and she was a relative. It should be easy. In the last ten minutes, she'd become an amazingly accomplished liar.

But Drew was there. As soon as he heard her voice, he said, "We have nothing to talk about, Tori. I wish you every happiness." Then he hung up on her.

Faint heart never won fair son of Scotland, she told herself, and punched in his number again. When he answered, she explained everything in a rush of words, not giving him a chance to respond till she added, "So you can press charges against Mitch if you want to. He shouldn't be allowed to get away with what he did to you."

"I want to see you, Tori," Drew replied. "Let's forget about that egomaniac. He's out of our lives for good. Could you meet me at the Baxter Arms at noon tomorrow? I think of it as the place where I first knew I was in love with you."

"That was the day we met at the art gallery," she said, "in front of a field of buttercups."

"I remember that picture. A mother and daughter. I thought the mother looked just like you, Tori."

"I consider that a compliment. She was lovely. Make it 12:30 tomorrow, Drew. I'm off for a couple of days, so we'll have lots of time."

"You can bank on that. I'm going to finish my column today and take tomorrow off do we can have the whole day together."

Tori was already deciding what to wear as she headed into the shower to shampoo her hair. She felt as though a great weight had been lifted from her shoulders. She felt glad to be alive.

32

Sometimes a Great Notion Comes in Red and Green

With perfect timing, they met outside the Baxter Arms at twelve-thirty the next day.

"Let's see if our table's available," said Andrew.

"You still remember where we sat?"

"I remember everything about that day. What you were wearing, how you looked, what you said."

"You're such a romantic, Drew."

"Guilty as charged."

They ordered a pasta dish with red wine and toasted each other over steaming plates. When they had finished eating, he poured more wine for them and raised his glass once again. "To my beautiful green-eyed girl. That sweater you're wearing matches your eyes, Tori. I can hardly believe we're actually here together again. It's like a dream come true. I'm so glad you broke your engagement."

She smiled. "Me, too. But it's going to be hard telling my family there isn't going to be a wedding after all."

"Maybe you won't have to tell them that. I'm yours if you'll have me. I love you, Tori. I know we could be happy."

She was silent for several seconds. "Come to think of it, Drew, I never told my family the name of my groom-to-be. Maybe that's some sort of omen that it was never meant to be Mitch Ames."

"You still haven't answered me. I know I'm not good looking but..."

Suddenly, she jumped up, and ignoring the other diners, moved to his side and kissed him full on the mouth. "You look good to me, Drew. Of course I'll marry you. The sooner, the better."

"So shall we leave here now and pick out a diamond for you—or go to my house and make love for the rest of the afternoon?"

"I opt for the latter," Tori replied, feeling herself blushing as she spoke. "Anyway, I don't want a diamond. I'd rather have an emerald, my birthstone."

"Mine's a ruby," he said. "We're red and green—like Christmas."

"Hey—we could have a Christmas wedding! Get all our relatives together for the holidays. Let's order some of Baxter's famous cheesecake now to have with our coffee. We need to start making plans."

"A Christmas wedding. What a good idea! How about December twentieth? An easy date for me to remember our anniversary each year."

She laughed. "Don't worry. I'll remind you."

"The Rose Room here will be perfect for our reception. One of my friends at the paper had his reception here. I was best man for him. Now he can do the same for me."

"My sister Rita and her husband Jason and their boys will be coming from San Francisco. Maybe we can talk their boys Donnie and David into being ring bearers for us. Rita's already agreed to be my matron-of-honor. And my dad's been looking forward to walking me down the aisle. Drew, how do you feel about tying the knot in the Unitarian church?

"I don't know very much about it, Tori. But we'll go wherever you want."

"Unitarians go back a long way. Thomas Jefferson was one. So was Ralph Waldo Emerson, to name just a couple of them. Our motto is 'You don't have to think alike in order to love alike.' We welcome everyone—agnostics and even atheists. And we have interesting guest speakers. Do you believe in God, Drew?"

"That's a pretty heavy question. I guess you could say I believe in TGM."

"What's that?"

"The Great Mystery."

"I'll buy that."

"Unitarianism sounds as though it has definite appeal for me, Tori. I was raised Presbyterian but I haven't been to church for years—except for the odd funeral or wedding."

"I was raised Anglican, but I got tired of all the kneeling and chanting, all the dogma. And I kept thinking about the wickedness of Henry the Eighth in founding it."

He chuckled. "I suppose we're all on a spiritual journey of some sort. But beheading wives shouldn't be part of it."

"The Reverend Dawson's a kindly old soul. Very open-minded. You'll like him. He'll even let us write our own vows if we want."

"Sounds good to me. Oh, Tori, I can't wait for us to be together. Let's hope our families find the date acceptable. My parents have already made their annual visit from Scotland, but I'm sure they'll be happy to come back for this occasion. They've been thinking of moving to Canada when my dad retires, and when they meet you I'll bet that cinches it."

"What does your dad do?"

"He's a doctor. A pediatrician. My parents both wanted me to follow in his footsteps, but I had my own ideas. I was born ten years after they married, and they called me their miracle baby. Maybe that's why I found mother love becoming smother love. I decided I had to get away. Far away. I do love them though—if my dad's a bit of an autocrat and my mother never stops talking."

Tori smiled. My stepmother's the same. I don't think Nora's ever had an unexpressed thought in her life. But she makes my dad happy. That's all that matters to me."

"I can't wait to see our two mothers together. Should be fun. Verbal warfare. We can put up all our family members between us. Your parents can stay with you, Tori, and I'll take Rita and her family along with my folks at my house."

"Is it boy proof? Their sons are nine and seven."

He chuckled. "No problem. I like kids. This way our relatives will really get to know each other."

Tori sighed. "I wish you could meet my brother Billy. He's in Haiti doing what he can to help down there. He sent me a wedding gift already—a beautiful hand-carved wooden mask depicting Comedy and Tragedy."

"After that terrible earthquake and the cholera epidemic, those people need all the help they can get. He must be very dedicated."

"It wasn't totally altruistic on his part," Tori confessed. "He went because the girl of his dreams was going."

"Did he win her?"

"He told me he's making some headway. Billy's more like me than my sister Rita. He and I are pretty liberal. Rita and her husband Jason are staunch Republicans. Better steer clear of politics with them. I always do."

"Politics and religion are always good subjects to avoid. It will be great celebrating the holidays together. I'll cook a turkey with all the trimmings."

"What about our honeymoon?"

"Tori, every day with you will be a honeymoon for me. Now let's get out of here and have our first undress rehearsal."

33
Victoria Meets Tuxedo the Cat

TORI'S FIRST SIGHT OF ANDREW'S HOUSE came as a pleasant surprise. A large red brick, ranch style bungalow surrounded by spruce trees—again, she thought, the colors of Christmas. The more she thought about a Yuletide wedding, the more the idea appealed to her.

Inside, the house was a disaster. Reflective, she decided, of a man living alone. But she saw immediately that the open concept plan had possibilities. All it needed was a woman's touch. She was glad she was going to be that woman.

"I tried to tidy up a bit," Andrew remarked, "but it's still rather a mess, isn't it. I do have a cleaning lady come once a week, but she's been sick with the flu."

"Is she a redhead?" Tori asked.

"What's that?"

"Just a little joke. I'll let you in on it later."

"You can make any changes you want to, Tori. Home décor is not one of my talents."

"You're a talented writer. That's enough. I can see you writing a novel someday. Do your parents approve of your career choice now?"

"They seem to. I e-mail my columns to them and they must be pleased because they pass them along to friends. What would you like to drink? I have tea, coffee, juice—and I think I have a bottle of Merlot somewhere."

"Isn't that the wine they made fun of in that film Sideways?"

"It is, but I don't care. I like it."

"Well, pour me a glass and I'll see if it's as good as the red house wine we had at the Baxter Arms."

Tori crossed the room to settle into the brown plaid sofa on one side of the fireplace. This monstrosity, she said to herself, will be the first thing to go. And that orange corduroy basket chair will be next.

All at once, something brushed by Tori's legs. She gave a cry of alarm that brought Drew running.

"It's a cat!" she exclaimed. "I didn't know you had a cat."

Drew smiled. "Now you know. Tuxedo, meet Miss Victoria Walker. I hope you're not allergic to pets."

"No, I'm not. I like cats. Where did you get him?"

"He got me. Came to our door a couple of years ago looking half starved. My girlfriend didn't want to let him in, but I did. It was a cold night and he looked hungry. Luckily, we had a can of tuna in the cupboard. I put an ad in the paper the next day, but nobody claimed him."

Tori leaned down to pick up the big black and white cat. He stared up, his big green eyes appraising her. "Cats always look as though they're trying out their eyes for the very first time," she said.

Andrew laughed. "Exactly. He doesn't miss much with those orbs."

As she stroked the big tom, he began to purr like a small motor. Tori was delighted. "I've always wanted a pet," she said, "but we weren't allowed to have them in the apartment building."

"My girlfriend pretty much ignored him," Drew said. "I guess she didn't like pets any more than she liked the idea of having children."

"So there was no fight over custody of Tuxedo when you two parted company."

"No fight over anything. It was amicable on both sides. I even helped her with some stuff when she moved out of town."

"That sounds like you, Drew. Now how about those drinks?"

They took sips of wine and set their glasses on the black wooden coffee table in front of them.

"Merlot is good," she said, "wine snobs notwithstanding."

"You're good," he said, taking her into his arms. He looked for long seconds into her eyes before kissing her, gently at first, then with urgency.

"Not here," she murmured. "Let's go to your bedroom."

With strength that took her by surprise, Drew picked her up and carried her into the master bedroom. They undressed each other, kissing often. "You're exactly the right height for me to nuzzle against your neck," he whispered. "You're so beautiful, Tori. So very beautiful."

"My breasts are too small."

"Your breasts are perfect. You're perfect. I wouldn't change a single thing about you."

"Except my marital status," she teased.

"Right."

They tumbled into bed and he found her more than ready to accept him.

Two minutes later, he was apologizing. "I'm so sorry, Tori. I couldn't hold back. I've dreamt about this so often. Next time will be better. I promise you."

They lay side by side, discussing their wedding plans. "We'll have lots of arrangements to make," she said. "We'll have to call our families first thing in the morning."

"And book the Rose Room," he added, "if all goes well. It's small, only holds about fifty people, but they'll have a Christmas tree in one corner. They go all out on decorations."

"Good. A Christmas tree to put our wedding gifts under. Six toasters and half a dozen electric kettles."

He laughed. "You're such fun to be with, Tori. We're going to have a good life." He snuggled close to her, nibbling her ear lobe. "You and I and Zoe and Zak. Yes, you told me about those names. I like Zoe—it's the Greek word for life. Zak, I'm not so sure about."

"Well, if we have a boy, I'll let you name him."

"How about John Andrew Macdonald? Then he can be John A.—like our first prime minister. I've been meaning to ask you. Are you keeping your maiden name or hyphening the two or what?"

"I like the sound of Victoria Macdonald. It's euphonius. Our two last names would be cumbersome. My dad's a bit old-fashioned. He'll approve of my choice. He wants to pay for my wedding and we'll have to let him. He can well afford it."

"What will he think of our Christmas motif?"

"He'll like it. So will Nora. I'll wear the traditional white dress and carry red roses with lots of green leaves, so I'll be a true Christmas bride."

"And I'll be a true husband—forever. For more red, you can wear those sexy high heels of yours—the ones you wore at Bella's party."

"I'll be miles taller than you in them!"

"Who cares? I don't. I just remembered—I have a Hunter green suit. Quite a dark shade. I've hardly ever worn it. I'll buy a red tie to go with it."

"We'll decorate the church with poinsettias. It'll be the ultimate in Noel Nuptials—music, scented candles and all."

"We'll encourage our guests to wear something red or green. Max and Derek will love it. We are inviting them, aren't we? And my friends at the paper are good sports. They'll go along with the idea, I'm sure."

"So will my friends from the hospital."

"I'd like to invite a couple of my buddies from our baseball team."

"You play baseball?"

"Every summer. We're called the Sunfield Sluggers."

"Drew, there's so much I don't know about you. For instance, when's your birthday? Mine's May the twenty-first. I'm a Gemini. I'm twenty-seven."

"Mine's July twenty-fourth. I'm a Leo. I'll be thirty next year."

"So we're getting married while you're still in your twenties."

"Right. And before the New Year. Think of the tax break!"

"I can't think at all with you kissing my neck and running your hands all over me. Not that I want you to stop."

He moved down the length of her body, kissing every inch of it and murmuring endearments all the while. After half an hour of foreplay, he entered her again, and true to his promise, the second time was better. Far better.

When they finally left the bedroom and moved to the kitchen, she was wearing Drew's white terrycloth robe, and he was keeping warm in his beige gabardine raincoat. He made them cheese, mushroom, onion, and red pepper omelets. They ate ravenously in the dining area, while listening to one of his CDs. Louis Armstrong was declaring it a wonderful world. Tori couldn't have agreed more.

"I've always wanted a man who can cook," she confessed, slathering a piece of multi-grain toast with marmalade. That was delicious, Drew."

"I have a limited repertoire in the kitchen. But I make a mean omelet—if I do say so myself."

Tori broke her overnight rule by staying the night, and the third time they made love was the best of all.

34
Jingle Bells and Wedding Bells

THEIR WEDDING DAY DAWNED WITHOUT A CLOUD in the bright blue sky. Tori leaned back against the plush upholstery of the Cadillac her father had rented for this special occasion. She was still amazed at how smoothly their arrangements had worked out. Not that it wasn't chaotic when they were all together at Drew's and at the rehearsal. But it was a happy kind of chaos. She was so certain she was doing the right thing she wasn't nearly as nervous as she'd expected to be.

From the front seat of the car, Nora turned her head and continued her incessant chatter. "Rita's looking well, isn't she? Jason's aged a lot since I last saw him. And he's put on too much weight. The boys are darling little lads, so cute in those rented tuxedos. You look lovely, Tori. The dress is flattering on a tall girl. I'm glad you decided to wear flats. This way you won't tower over everybody in the pictures. Drew's parents are really nice, but doesn't his mother ever stop talking? I can hardly get a word in edgewise with her. His dad's on the quiet side, but I don't think he's unfriendly. Maybe he just doesn't get a chance to express himself with such a motor-mouth for a wife."

Tori let the flow of words wash over her, amused at their irony. She thought of Robert Burns; "O would the genie some power give us, to see ourselves as others see us." Or something like that. She wasn't sure of the word 'genie'. She was still pondering it when they arrived at the church and her dad was able to manage a few words.

"Here we are. Look! The sun has come out—just for you, Princess."

Tall Stuff

The old term of endearment from her childhood almost brought tears to Tori's eyes. A light coating of snow lay on the ground, sparkling in the sunlight like jeweled icing sugar.

Silver-haired Reverend Dawson was ready for them, long scarlet and emerald scarves adorning his white surplice. He'd even pinned a sprig of holly on one of them, getting completely into the spirit of a Yuletide wedding. Rita was wearing a moss-green silk dress and a big smile for her little sister. Tori marveled at how much she resembled their petite blonde mother. Her boys, Donnie and David, stood bearing red and green satin cushions holding the gold wedding bands. Millie had finished making the cushions just in time for the ceremony. Then Tori turned to Drew, and she had eyes only for him.

When the time came for their vows, Drew surprised her by beginning his with Ruth's words to Naomi in the Old Testament of the Bible. "Wither thou goest, I will go," he said, "and where thou lodgest, I will lodge. Thy people shall be my people, and thy God, my God. I love you, Victoria Jane Walker, and I will always put you first in my life, as long as we both shall live."

Tori forgot the vows she had memorized and repeated his promise back to him, almost word for word.

There was a moment of panic when Donnie dropped his red cushion and Drew's ring rolled away.

"Sorry, Sis," Rita murmured.

"Not to worry. Every wedding has to have at least one little glitch."

Max found the ring under his pew and returned it to the distraught little boy. All went smoothly for the rest of the nuptials and Drew took his time with their first kiss as man and wife. He even had the audacity to give her lips a little lick with his tongue at the end of it.

The December sun was still shining brightly when they left the church to go to the reception in the Rose Room. A good omen, thought Tori, soaking up the rays of the great star's blessing. Happy the bride the sun shines on. She squeezed Drew's hand as he turned to her and declared, "I'm the luckiest man in the world."

Andrew had prevailed upon friends of his to provide live music for them, and the trio—piano, drums, and sax, created danceable sounds even though they were only amateur musicians. As he took her into his arms for their first dance as husband and wife, Drew held her close and they moved gracefully across the floor. At the head table, their fathers chatted about world soccer and their mothers chatted non-stop about everything, each trying to win the battle of words.

Tori glanced around, pleased at the way many of their guests had entered into the Christmas spirit by donning red Santa hats or the green pointed ones of his elves, Kate and Millie and their husbands among them. Mary Alice wore a sparkling ruby headband and Allen a bright green tie. Their wedding pictures would be beautiful.

Before the evening ended, Max claimed her for a dance. "You are one gorgeous bride, Tall Stuff," he remarked. "I'm glad you chose the right groom. Say, I'm directing a play in March. If you come and read you won't have to worry about running into Mitch Ames. I hear he went back to Edmonton some time ago."

"So that's why our paths haven't crossed," she said. "Not that I wanted them to."

"It's a drama this time. There's a role that would be perfect for you. You've got talent, Tori. It'll be a good production."

"Thanks, Max, but I'm hoping to have my own production underway by March."

For a moment, he looked puzzled. Then he laughed. "I get it, Tori. And I wish you luck."

"Who are you dating these days, Max?"

"Derek."

"What!"

"I decided it was high time I came out of the closet. I'm bi-sexual, but I've never acted on it. I made Derek go to a dentist, and his breath's no longer a problem. Actually, he's a sweet guy and good company. The best. And he's as passionate about the theatre as I am. I think we'll make a go of it as a couple."

"I wish you both all the best, Max. If you're half as happy as I am, you'll have it made."

When the reception wound down, Tori and Drew retired to a room they'd booked in the Baxter Arms, leaving their families the keys to their separate domiciles. Drew's father promised he'd look after their gifts for them.

Tall Stuff

"Let them work out their own sleeping arrangements," said Andrew. "We need this night all to ourselves. The champagne's waiting in the ice bucket."

"I don't need it to feel high," said Tori. "I'm high on love."

"Who needs bubbly," he agreed. "I'm roaring drunk on the deep green sea of your fantastic eyes."

"Andrew Ian Macdonald, you have the soul of a poet."

"Thank you, Mrs. Macdonald. Now let's draw the curtains and begin our first act as man and wife."

35

Valentines, Roses, and Raging Snowstorms

VALENTINE'S DAY brought with it the first real blizzard of the year. Tori was glad she didn't have to work. She hated winter driving. The slightest bit of fishtailing had her heart pounding and her hold on the steering wheel becoming a death grip.

It didn't seem to bother Andrew. "That was the first thing I had to get used to when I moved to Canada," he'd told her. "Now I don't mind the great Canadian winter. It's the idiots who think they can speed the way they do in the other three seasons that bug me."

So Tori wasn't too surprised when he called and said he was setting out to cover a human interest story in Ironwood, a little hamlet on the river fourteen miles from Sunfield. She was worried though. She'd heard of cars sliding off the road in bad conditions and ending up in the river. Hypothermia could kill a person fast.

She'd better keep busy, she told herself. Drew had promised her he'd be home by five o'clock. She'd have time to make his favorite dinner—baked ham, scalloped potatoes, glazed baby carrots, and a tossed garden salad. Cherry cheesecake for dessert. A special dessert for Valentine's Day. She had his card all ready. It had been a thrill to pick out one with the words: TO MY HUSBAND. Inside, she'd written even more special words, telling him the good news that either Zoe or John A. was on the way. She had taken the pregnancy test twice to be absolutely certain.

As she peeled half a dozen potatoes, Tori tried to keep from looking out the kitchen window above the sink. The storm seemed to be getting worse by the minute. A sharp wind had come up, setting the house to creaking ominously. What kind of story could be worth driving out of town for in this weather?

An hour later, Tori pulled the roaster out of the oven and inspected the clove-studded ham. It smelled good to her. So had her breakfast that morning. Maybe she'd be one of the lucky ones and not suffer from morning sickness.

At four-thirty, the front doorbell rang. Who could be calling in this storm? she wondered. Then a terrible fear clutched her. Maybe it was the police coming to tell her there'd been an accident. She should have known her life was too perfect to last, too good to be true. Trembling, she went to answer the summons.

A teen-aged delivery boy presented her with a large, well-wrapped bouquet of red roses. She almost fainted with relief. "Drive carefully," she called out as he left, her voice barely audible above the gale-force wind.

As she filled a large cut-glass vase with water, a wedding present from Kate, Tori chastised herself for letting her imagination run away with her. Drew was a good driver. He'd take his time. He'd be fine.

She set the vase on the gleaming mahogany dining room table beside the propped-up Valentine for Drew and picked up the card tucked into the roses. It read, "For my Forever Sweetheart, with a lifetime of love, Drew."

Tori decided she needed a cup of tea. Maybe it would calm her nerves. It seemed to work for the British in stressful times. She put on a CD and settled with her Red Rose tea in the white leather armchair on one side of their fireplace. Drew would make them a fire when he got home. She leaned back, listening as a female voice filled the room with the words, "I love Paris in the springtime." She and Drew had loved it in the wintertime. They'd gone there for a couple of days in January, calling it a honeymoon. So what if it was only Paris, Ontario? They'd always be able to tell their children they'd honeymooned in Paris. They'd promised each other they would visit the real City of Eternal Light to celebrate their Silver Anniversary.

When the music ended, Tori picked up a copy of Chatelaine from the basket beside her chair and tried to read. It was useless. She couldn't ignore the curtains of snow obliterating the picture window. Images of cars skidding into ditches kept flashing on her mind screen. Cars flipping over, wheels spinning upside down as they sank into the frigid waters of the river. She knew she shouldn't call him when he was on the road, but she couldn't help herself. She went to the kitchen and punched in the number of his cell phone. No answer. She looked up at the kitchen clock. Five-twenty. Twenty minutes late was nothing to worry about in this kind of storm, she told herself. He'd probably forgotten to re-charge his phone. If only she could talk to him! She jumped when the phone rang ten minutes later. It was only a telemarketing call, but it took her several minutes to calm down.

By six-fifteen, Tori was frantic. She began pacing the length of the living room, staring out the window each time she passed it. Even Tuxedo the cat seemed perturbed. He kept running back and forth from the door to her. She should have known her life was too perfect, should have known such happiness was never meant for her. How could she go on living if something had happened to Drew? Life without him was unthinkable. She almost wept with relief when, at six-thirty, she heard a car pull into their driveway. She raced to the front door and flung it open. His green Buick was white with snow.

Grinning hugely, Drew came breezing in, snowflakes clinging to his thick blonde hair. "I tried to call but my phone was dead. I'd forgotten to re-charge it. Sorry I'm a bit late. Hope you weren't worried."

Before she had time to reply, before he even took off his coat, he was thrusting a large package into her hands.

"Your Valentine gift," he said. "Something I've been after for weeks. Go on—open it."

"The buttercup picture!" she cried, tearing away the brown paper wrapping. "How did you get it? The last time we went to look at it, it had been sold."

"I tracked down the man who bought it. He lives in Ironwood. It wasn't easy, but I persuaded him to let me buy it from him."

"So that was your human interest story!"

"I wanted it, Tori. For us. And I wanted to give it to you today."

"It is beautiful, Drew. The mother and child look so eternally happy."

"It will always remind me of the day I fell in love with you."

Tori set the picture down and reached under his cold black overcoat to hold him close. "I have a Valentine surprise for you too. It's in your card on the dining room table, right beside the lovely roses you sent."

Moments later, Drew was dancing her around that table, dancing to music only the two of them could hear.

A Short Bio

Norma West Linder was born in Toronto, spent her childhood on Manitoulin Island, and teenage years in Muskoka. She is a member of, The Writers' Union of Canada, The Ontario Poetry Society, WITS (Writers International Through Sarnia) and Past President of the Sarnia Branch of the Canadian Authors Assoc.

Linder is the author of 5 novels, 14 collections of poetry, a memoir of Manitoulin Island, two children's books, and a biography of Pauline McGibbon. For 24 years she was on the faculty of Lambton College in Sarnia, teaching English and Creative Writing, retiring in 1992. For 7 years she wrote a monthly column for the Sarnia Observer. Her short stories have been published internationally and broadcast on the CBC. Her poetry has been published in, Fiddlehead, White Wall Review, Room of One's Own, Quills, Prairie Journal, FreeFall Magazine, Mobius, and other periodicals. In 2006 she compiled and edited Enchanted Crossroads for The Ontario Poetry Society. Her latest publications are collections of poems entitled, When Angels Weep, Lovely as a Tree, and Adder's Tongues. A collection of her short stories was released in August of 2013, entitled No Common Thread, published by Hidden Brook Press. In 2014, Two Paths Through the Seasons, a poetry book featuring Linder and James Deahl was published in Israel. In 2016, Hidden Brook Press published, The Pastel Planet, a children's book. Her poem "Valediction" was set to music by composer Jeffrey Ryan, performed in Toronto by the Tefelmusik Baroque Orchestra.

She lives in Sarnia, Ontario with poet James Deahl. When not writing, Linder enjoys reading, swimming, and photography. She has two daughters and a son.

Hidden Brook Press books by Norma West Linder:

No Common Thread, The Selected Short Fiction of Norma West Linder
ISBN – 978-1-897475-91-1

The Pastel Planet: A Manitoulin Island Adventure
ISBN – 978-1-927725-24-5

Tall Stuff
ISBN – 978-1-927725-38-2

All three of these books are available at e-stores around the world, including, Amazon, Barnes & Noble and Indigo. Books can also be ordered from www.HiddenBrookPress.com

Check each e-store for the best price on book and shipping as prices tend to vary from store to store.